D0401076

Dawn on the Coast

THE BABY-SITTERS CLUB®

Dawn on the Coast

ANN M. MARTIN

SCHOLASTIC INC.

The author would like to thank
Jan Carr for her help in writing this book.

Copyright © 1989 by Ann M. Martin

This book was originally published in paperback by Scholastic Inc. in 1989.

All rights reserved. Published by Scholastic Inc., *Publishers since 1920*. SCHOLASTIC, THE BABY-SITTERS CLUB, and associated logos are trademarks and/or registered trademarks of Scholastic Inc.

The publisher does not have any control over and does not assume any responsibility for author or third-party websites or their content.

No part of this publication may be reproduced, stored in a retrieval system, or transmitted in any form or by any means, electronic, mechanical, photocopying, recording, or otherwise, without written permission of the publisher. For information regarding permission, write to Scholastic Inc., Attention: Permissions Department, 557 Broadway, New York, NY 10012.

ISBN 978-1-338-81497-2

10 9 8 7 6 5 4 3 2 1   23 24 25 26 27

Printed in the U.S.A. 40
This edition first printing 2023

Book design by Maeve Norton

CHAPTER 1

Dear Sunshine,

The countdown is on. Only a few days left until you get on that plane and land in beautiful, <u>sunny</u> California. I can't wait to see you, sweetie. And Jeff is so excited, you'd think it was Christmas morning. California, here you come! See you Sunday night at the airport.

Love and a big hug,
Dad

A trip to the West Coast. It was the highlight of my spring, that's for sure. When I got to California, I had an absolutely fantastic time. So how come I ended up feeling so confused? Believe me, there's a lot to tell. And I might as well start at the beginning.

First off, you're probably wondering who Sunshine is. Well, that's me. Of course nobody around here calls me Sunshine. Here in Connecticut they call me by my regular name, Dawn Schafer. But not my dad. He started calling me Sunshine when I was little and, unfortunately, it stuck. Maybe he gave me the name because of my long blonde hair. My hair is so light it's almost the color of cornsilk, and it reaches all the way past my waist. Or maybe Dad gave me the name because I love the sun so much. I really do. I love warm weather and the beach.

I guess I'm just a California girl at heart. After all, that's where I came from. And that Sunday, I was getting to go back for a visit!

I got the postcard from Dad when I came home from school that Thursday afternoon. I still had so much to do, so much to get ready. I dragged my suitcase out of the closet, threw it on the bed, and started to lay out my clothes. I decided to bring my white cotton skirt — I could wear that with anything. And, of course, my bathing suit (a bikini) and my jeans and sneakers. I wasn't sure about my yellow cotton overalls. And would I really need *three* sundresses?

2

Maybe you're wondering why my dad lives in California and I live in Connecticut. Well, sometimes I wonder, too. Believe me, it's not the way I would've arranged it. But even so, things are working out okay. You see, about a year and a half ago, Mom and Dad got divorced. Dad stayed in our house in California and Mom moved me and my brother, Jeff, here to Stoneybrook, Connecticut. I think Mom wanted to come here because my grandparents live here and it's the town where she grew up. To tell the truth, at first I wasn't the happiest, but then I adjusted. I found myself a best friend, Mary Anne Spier, and I got invited to join the Baby-sitters Club, which is just about the most fun club in the whole wide world.

My brother, Jeff, though, didn't adjust so easily. In fact, he didn't adjust at all. He started getting kind of nasty with me and Mom, and he even started to get in fights at school. It was pretty bad. His teacher kept calling up Mom and I don't think Mom knew what to do. Finally we decided to let Jeff go back to California for awhile. He really just wanted to be back with his friends and live with Dad. I don't think Mom was thrilled with the idea, but she figured she had to let Jeff try it for six months.

Me, I didn't like the idea at all. It was bad enough that Mom and Dad had to get divorced. Already our family was split. But when Jeff left Mom and me, too, it felt like Jeff was up and deserting us. And then another part of me thought, hey, why couldn't *I* be the one to get to move back to California?

Now I'm kind of used to the idea. In my head I understand all the reasons why things are the way they are. But sometimes it does seem strange the way the family has divided up. Boys against the girls. Or West Coast against the East Coast. I love Mom, and she and I get to stay together, but of course I love Dad and Jeff, and I miss them sometimes. And I know they miss us, too.

But Mom is the greatest. She and I have gotten a lot closer through all of this and we've made a whole new life for ourselves. We live in an old, old farmhouse that was built in 1795. No kidding. The rooms are really small and the doorways are so short that tall people have to stoop to get through them. Mom says people used to be shorter in the 1700s.

The best thing about our house, though, is that it has a secret trapdoor in our barn that leads into a long, dark tunnel. You need a flashlight to walk through. The tunnel leads up into our house and comes out . . . right at the wall to my bedroom! The wall has a special latch that springs open to the touch. Talk about exciting. You should've seen the faces on my friends in the Baby-sitters Club when I showed them.

Maybe I should tell you a little bit about the club. There're six of us in it now, and we also have two associate members. What it is is just what it says, a club for baby-sitters. It was Kristy Thomas's great idea. She's our president. She figured that it would be great if there was a club that all the parents in the neighborhood could use whenever they needed a sitter. That way, they'd be pretty sure of getting someone for the job and they'd only have to make one call. Great for them, and great for us, too, since we're all super sitters and we love the work. Leave it to Kristy to come up with a good business idea. And leave it to Kristy to organize the whole thing.

What we do is this: Three times a week we have meetings in the afternoon. We meet at Claudia's house because she has a phone in her room . . . with her very own number! Claudia is Claudia Kishi and she's our vice-president. Claudia is about as different from Kristy as you can get. Kristy is kind of small for her age and is a real tomboy. She always wears the same thing — jeans, a turtle neck, and sneakers. But not Claudia. You can always count on Claudia to be wearing some really unusual outfit, like a white jumpsuit with a wide purple belt and purple high-top sneakers. Claudia's Japanese American and she's got beautiful, long, shiny black hair that she fixes differently practically every day. She loves art, too, so she has a really interesting sense of style.

After those two, there's Mary Anne Spier, our club secretary, and, as I said, she's my best friend in Stoneybrook. Mary Anne lives alone with her father because her mother died when she was a baby. Her father's been kind of strict with her and a lot of people think Mary Anne's quiet. It's true, she can be shy sometimes. But wouldn't you know it, she was the first one of us to get a boyfriend!

Speaking of boyfriends, when I first moved to Stoneybrook and became friends with Mary Anne, we found out something really exciting — my mom and Mary Anne's dad used to go out together in high school! Then, for a while, they even started going out together again! Imagine. My mom going with my best friend's dad. Mary Anne and I were in seventh heaven. We were hoping our parents might even get *married* to each other. That would've made Mary Anne and me sisters! Now things have cooled off a little, but as Mary Anne says, you never know. . . .

So that's part of the club. Kristy, Claudia, Mary Anne, and I are all in eighth grade, so we are *very* experienced sitters. We used to have another eighth-grade member, Stacey, but she moved back to New York City, which was really sad, so we had to get someone to fill Stacey's place in the club. That's where Mallory and Jessi come in. Mallory and Jessi are our sixth-grade members. They can't sit at nighttime, except for their own brothers and sisters, but both of them are really good. We know Mallory really well because we baby-sit for her family, the Pikes. The Pikes have eight kids, and since Mallory is the oldest, she used to help us out.

Jessi is Mallory's friend and she's a newcomer to Stoneybrook. Her family is one of the first Black families in the neighborhood, so I think that in the beginning, Jessi felt a little strange. When she first moved here, she wasn't even sure she wanted to continue with her ballet lessons, and she is a really talented ballet dancer — long-legged and graceful.

Wow! When I think about it, I do have a nice bunch of friends in Stoneybrook. As I was packing that day, I also started thinking about my friends in California. Clover and Daffodil (those are the kids I used to baby-sit for) and, of course, Sunny, who had been my best friend in California since second grade. That reminded me — I'd better stick suntan lotion in my suitcase. Sunny and I would probably want to go to the beach one day. Then I started making a list of all the other cosmetics and things I would need.

Just then my mom came home. She usually doesn't get home from work until 5:45 or so, but that day she was early.

"Hi, Dawn!" she called up the stairs.

I could hear her kick off her shoes in the living room, drop her purse on the couch and her keys on the kitchen table. That's my mom, all right. I love her, but she is a little on the disorganized side. Mom padded up the stairs and plunked herself down on the one corner of my bed that wasn't covered with stuff.

"What's this?" she said, picking up my list. When she saw what it was, she laughed. "I guess you didn't learn that from your old mother," she said.

It's true. If Mom ever bothered to make a list, she'd probably just lose it.

"How was work today?" I asked her.

Mom sighed and looked vaguely across the bed at all my things.

"You're going to have such a good time," she said.

I suddenly realized that when I went off to California, Mom was going to be left all alone in Stoneybrook.

"Mom, are you going to be all right?" I asked. "I mean, all alone?"

She tucked her legs under her, like she had so many times lately when we found ourselves sitting in my room talking.

"Of course I am, sweetie," she said. "What? Are you worried about me? Don't worry. I've got Granny and Pop-Pop while you're gone. And Trip's already asked me out to dinner. . . ."

"The Trip-Man!" I groaned. Trip is a man who was dating my mother. I call him the Trip-Man. He's a real conservative type. Tortoiseshell glasses, you know what I mean. How could I leave Mom alone with *him?*

"Mom," I said, "I feel kind of funny going off to be with Dad and Jeff, and you having to stay here."

"It's only for your spring vacation," she said. "Besides, think of what an adventure I'm going to have without you. I'll probably misplace my keys and not find them the whole time you're away. And when I go out with Trip, I'll probably end up wearing one brown shoe and one red."

I threw my arms around Mom and gave her a quick kiss.

"Oh, Mom," I said. "I'm so glad that you and I stuck together. What if you were here and I was there? What if the family was even more split up than it is now? I'll never leave you. Never."

Mom didn't answer me, she just stared across my bed at the suitcase and all my clothes. Her eyes got a little misty, but right away she turned to me and said, "You didn't start anything for dinner yet, did you?"

Weekday dinners are usually my job.

"Not yet," I said. "I was thinking maybe barley casserole . . ."

"Let's go out," Mom said suddenly. "What do you say? We'll go to Cabbages and Kings and have one of those wonderful tofu dinners."

"Or the avocado salad," I said.

"Aaaah, avocado . . ." My mother closed her eyes at the thought. "Think of all those wonderful California avocados you're going to be gobbling down soon. Come on. Let's go celebrate. Avocados, here we come."

I grabbed my sweater and Mom stood up, puzzled, and glanced around the floor.

"Where're my shoes?" she said.

"Living room," I answered.

Mom fumbled in her pockets for her keys.

"Your keys are on the kitchen table," I said. "And your purse is on the couch."

Mom looked a little sheepish.

"What am I going to do without you?" she laughed. "You have to admit. We make a good team."

We walked down the stairs, gathered up Mom's things, and headed out the door. When I got home that night I would have to finish packing my things. But, for then, I left them strewn across my bed. It wasn't every night that Mom and I could decide to drop everything and go to Cabbages and Kings for a close, warm mother-daughter meal. And besides, on Sunday I'd be leaving Stoneybrook for two whole weeks.

CHAPTER 2

Friday

Dear Dad and Jeff,

    Only two more days to C-Day!
That's what I'm calling my trip to
California now, and I can't, CAN'T WAIT
to see you. This'll have to be short
and sweet because I'm rushing off to a
slumber party at Kristys' house. All my
Baby-sitters Club friends will be there,
and I can't be late, since the whole
thing is a good-bye party for...

                              Yours truly,
                              Dawn

What a party. I was the first one to get to
Kristy's that night and, when I arrived, things
were still a little quiet and calm. Kristy lives in a

mansion. No kidding. But you practically need a mansion to hold all her family. There's Kristy and her mom and three brothers, and then there's Watson Brewer, Kristy's stepdad. He and Kristy's mom got married last summer and he has two kids of his own. (They come to stay every other weekend.) That would be plenty, but there's also Boo-Boo, the cat, and Shannon, the puppy.

I knocked on the big wooden door and Kristy let me in. She was wearing her usual — jeans, sneakers, a turtleneck. (What did I tell you?) She shut the door quickly behind me, so that Shannon wouldn't escape. Shannon jumped up on me and licked my arms. She really is a great puppy. She's still young, so her paws are too big for her body.

"Hi, Shann," I said. I petted her soft head and scratched behind her ears.

The doorbell rang again.

"Move it, Shannon," said Kristy. "It's probably Mary Anne."

The madness had started. When Kristy opened the door, it wasn't Mary Anne at all. It was Karen and Andrew, Kristy's stepsister and stepbrother.

"We're here!" Karen shouted into the house. She dropped her overnight bag on the hallway floor. "Daddy! Everybody! Here we are!"

Karen is only six years old, but she's got lots of confidence and is never at a loss for words. Andrew looked up at me and smiled.

"Hi, Dawn," he said. "Are you baby-sitting us?"

Andrew's only four and sometimes I have baby-sat for him, although, of course, Kristy takes all the jobs in her own house if she can.

"Not this time, Andrew," I said. "But I think you are going to see lots of baby-sitters tonight."

"Hi, Karen. Hi, Andrew. Oh, hello, Dawn." Kristy's mother bustled into the room and gave Andrew and Karen each a warm hug and kiss. "Take your stuff up and stash it in your rooms," she said. "It's going to be a full house tonight. Kristy's expecting a few guests."

Karen bounded up the stairs with her suitcase and Andrew stumbled after her, trying to keep up.

Kristy put her hands over her ears. "Aughhh!" she cried. "It sounds like wild horses!"

The doorbell rang again. This time it *was* Mary Anne, and Claudia was right behind her.

"Come in, come in." Kristy opened the door a crack, then hustled them in, but Shannon was too quick for her. The frisky puppy darted between Claudia's legs and scampered right outside.

"Shannon!" Kristy called, and ran out to catch her.

While Kristy was chasing after Shannon, Mallory and Jessi arrived. Jessi saw what was happening and took a ballet leap into the yard, just as Shannon was about to run into the bushes.

"Gotcha!" she said as she grabbed Shannon's collar. We all started clapping and Jessi took a deep bow. *"Grand jeté,"* she smiled. "You just never know when one is going to come in handy."

Well, one crisis down, but another was on the way. While Kristy led Shannon back into the house, Karen came screaming down the stairs.

"Ben Brewer!" she shouted. "Ben Brewer! He's clanking his chains!"

For a six-year-old girl, Karen has one wild imagination. She's convinced there's a ghost in the house named Ben Brewer, and she tells stories about him all the time. As I looked up, Sam and Charlie were sneaking around the bend at the top of the steps. They're Kristy's older brothers. Sam is fifteen and Charlie's seventeen.

"Shhh," Sam whispered to Charlie. He slipped down the stairs after Karen, grabbed her up from behind, and lifted her over his head.

"Aughhh!" screamed Karen.

Mrs. Brewer stuck her head back into the room to see what was going on. David Michael, Kristy's brother who's seven, was right behind her.

"No horseplay on the stairs," said David Michael. (It was obviously a rule he had heard many times.)

"That's right," said Mrs. Brewer.

Just then, the front door opened behind us and bumped Claudia and Mary Anne on their backsides.

"Excuse me. Excuse me." Someone was pushing his way through the crowd. It was Watson Brewer, home from work. "Well," he said, as he took a look at the chaos that greeted him. "Five more daughters, huh? Where did I get them all? Hello, girls."

"Hi, Mr. Brewer," we chorused.

"All right. All right. That's enough," Kristy said suddenly. "Baby-sitters upstairs."

I'm surprised she didn't say, "Forward, march!" or "Single file!" (she did sound like General Kristy), but we all trooped up the stairs after her. We left Watson and Kristy's mom kissing hello in the hallway, with their kids and their animals chasing all around them.

"Phew!" Kristy said. She shut the door behind us. Mary Anne, Claudia, and I collapsed on the bed. Jessi and Mallory sat cross-legged on the floor. Kristy pulled up a chair. It looked just like a regular meeting of the Baby-sitters Club, only we were in Kristy's room, not Claudia's. Kristy picked up a clipboard and pencil and rapped on the arm of her chair.

"The meeting will now come to order," she said.

"Meeting!" Claudia cried. "Kristy, this isn't a meeting. It's a party."

I smiled at Mary Anne. Mary Anne is a good friend of Kristy's, but she knows how Kristy loves to be bossy.

"True," said Kristy. "It's not exactly a meeting. But we do have a few things to decide. Pizza, for instance. Do we want some? And, if so, what kind?"

"Pizza would be good," said Mary Anne. Mary Anne is always agreeable. "Does anyone else want pizza?"

"P-I-I-I-I-Z-Z-A-A!" said Claudia in a deep, rumbling voice. She sounded like Cookie Monster demanding cookies.

"That's three," said Kristy. "Dawn?"

"Do they have broccoli pizza?" I asked.

"Ew!" Kristy made a gagging face.

"It *is* Dawn's party," said Mary Anne. "I think we should do what she wants."

Claudia crinkled up her nose.

"If they do have broccoli, maybe they could put it on only *part* of the pizza," she said.

Claudia was more polite about it, but I think the idea of broccoli pizza was as weird-sounding to Claudia as it was to Kristy. I'm the only member of the club who really likes health food. Everybody else is happier with hamburgers and french fries. Especially Claudia. Claudia takes junk food to the extreme. She keeps her bedroom stocked with Ring Dings and Twinkies. In fact, right then she reached into the knapsack she had brought and pulled out . . . a handful of Tootsie Roll Pops.

"Tootsie Pops all around," she said, passing them out, "and a fruit roll for Dawn."

We all sucked on our treats while Kristy finished the pizza order. Half a pie with broccoli (if they had it), half plain, and one whole pie with the works — sausage, mushrooms, onions, peppers, and pepperoni.

"No anchovies!" everyone voted. For once we were all in agreement.

The rest of the party was just as crazy as the start. When the pizza was delivered, Sam brought it up to Kristy's room. He knocked on the door. "Pizza man," he called in. Kristy let him in and tore open the boxes.

"What'd they give us? What'd they give us?"

she said excitedly. "EW!!!!" Kristy jumped away from the boxes in disgust. We all crowded around to see. There, all over the tops of both pizzas, were worms! . . . Rubber worms. Sam's shoulders were shaking with laughter.

"SA-AM!" Kristy said hotly. We should've known Sam would pull something like that. Sam is one of the world's champion practical jokers. (By the way, underneath all the worms, the pizza place *had* sent my broccoli.)

After pizza we wheeled out the television and set up a movie.

Kristy had picked out the spookiest movie she could find at the store, *Fright Night at Spook Lake.* It was all about a ghost who haunts an old lakeside resort house. When Karen heard the TV on, she knocked on the door and asked if she could join us.

"Only if you don't get scared," said Kristy.

"Okay," Karen agreed. She climbed into Kristy's lap.

But when the ghost first came on the screen, Karen shrieked. "That's Ben!" she cried. "That's exactly what Ben Brewer looks like!"

"Karen!" Kristy said firmly. "There is *nothing* to be afraid of. Look at me. Am *I* afraid? Of course not. There's *nothing* to be afraid of."

Just then, in the movie, the resort house got strangely quiet. An eerie light filled the inn's reception room and a breeze rustled the curtains. A phone rang loudly — Riiiiing! — and at that moment, the real phone right outside Kristy's room rang, too! We all screamed and jumped a mile. Kristy gulped and looked at us. You could tell her heart was racing, and I think she didn't know whether to answer the phone or not, but she did.

"Oh," she said. "Hi, Nannie." She heaved a big sigh. "It's only my grandmother," she whispered to us. "Phew."

When the movie was finished, Kristy's mom came in to collect Karen and take her off to bed. We stayed up a long time after that. We pushed Kristy's bed out of the way and put our sleeping bags and bedding in a circle, so that all our heads met in the center. We just talked and laughed about school and about boys. Claudia got some pieces of paper from Kristy's desk and drew little caricatures of us all. When Jessi posed for hers, she sat on the floor, her legs stretched out on either side of her and her torso folded all the way over so her stomach was flat on the ground.

"Wow!" said Mary Anne.

I think by then we were all getting tired, but nobody wanted to admit it. We talked on, but one by one we started to drift off. Only Mary Anne lay wide awake beside me.

"In two days you'll be in California," she whispered to me.

"Yeah," I said. I didn't sound as excited as I thought I would. All of a sudden I was a little nervous about going. I looked around the room. Here I was, with all my best friends — especially Mary Anne.

It all felt so cozy and homey. It felt like . . . like a family.

"You'll be gone so *long*," Mary Anne whispered. "And you'll have so much fun you won't even *think* of us."

"Of course I will," I said. "You're my *friends*. Anyway, I'll be home before you know it."

"Well, call whenever you want," Mary Anne said. "And send me a postcard?" She took my hand and squeezed it.

"I'll send you a zillion." I squeezed her hand back.

My thoughts were all jumbled as we lay there in the dark. But the thoughts tumbled into dreams, and soon I was fast asleep.

CHAPTER 3

Sunday

Dear Mary Anne,

   Well, I told you I'd send a postcard, but bet you never thought it'd be so soon. Here I am on the airplane and we've only been "in flight" for fifteen minutes. Not much to report, but I can tell you anything you want to know about oxygen masks, flotation devices, or exit doors. (The stewardness who did the safety demonstration reminds me of a kewpie doll.) It's going to be a <u>long</u> flight.

                               Love,
                               Dawn

Long flight was right. Long morning, too. That morning I woke up really early, a half an hour before my alarm. My brain was racing with all the things I needed for my trip: toothbrush, toothpaste, swimsuit, airplane ticket. I even wondered if maybe I had gotten the ticket wrong. Maybe I was supposed to fly out tomorrow, not today. It surprised me that I was so jittery. I've flown plenty of times before. But that morning, when my alarm went off, believe me, I was wide awake.

I could hear Mom in the shower, so I went down to fix myself a quick breakfast. There was granola in the cupboard, but no milk in the refrigerator. I poured myself a bowl and wondered if maybe I could substitute orange juice for milk. I decided to eat it plain.

Getting Mom to an airport in time is no small task. She thinks you don't have to get there until five minutes before flight time.

"They're always late," she says. "We'll just have to sit there."

Me, I like to count on an extra forty-five minutes to an hour. What if there's a traffic jam? And airlines overbook all the time. I could hear Mom singing away in the shower. I decided to knock on the door.

"In a minute, honey," she said.

It seemed like forever to me, but finally we were both showered, dressed, and out of the house. Mom had had her coffee and we had found her keys and I double-checked the things I had stuck in my carry-on bag: a favorite collection of ghost stories (*Spirits, Spooks, and Ghostly Tales*), some magazines, and some cards to write my friends. Since this wasn't a night flight, and since I would be on the plane for practically six whole hours, I figured I'd better come aboard with a few things to do.

On the ride to the airport, Mom let me listen to my radio station and didn't even ask me to turn it down. She didn't say an awful lot during the drive. Every once in awhile, she'd pop in with, "You remembered your underwear?" or, "Now don't forget your manners. 'Please, thank you.' . . . What am I saying? You know how to behave."

I think Mom was just nervous. I noticed that as she drove, her fingers kept kneading the steering wheel.

When we got to the airport, Mom found a spot in short-term parking. Then we went in, checked my suitcase, got me a window seat, and went to wait at the gate. I started to feel as choked up as Mom looked. I glanced at her, and she gave a half smile, and then her eyes welled up and over.

"Are you going to be okay, Mom?" I asked. Now I was beginning to cry.

"Oh, Dawn," she said. "I'm all right. I'm fine. You'd think I was sending you to Egypt or something."

When it came time for me to board, Mom walked me to the door and gave me a big hug.

"See you soon," I said.

She kissed my cheek. "Right," she said, awfully quickly.

I got on the plane and distracted myself with settling in. I wanted to make sure to get myself a pillow and a blanket. I wanted to check out the magazines that were on board — *Forbes*, *Business Week* . . . nothing for me. I guess I was starting to feel a little better because when the Kewpie doll stewardess gave her safety demonstration, I even found myself giggling. But when the plane started to taxi down the runway, I suddenly thought of Mom. I pictured her back in the parking lot trying to remember where she had parked the car.

"Row C," I thought, trying to send her the message. "Row C."

The plane took off and tears spilled down my cheeks. I was going to California. And Mom was going to be all alone.

Well, if it weren't for that stewardess, I might've cried the whole way out. I certainly wouldn't have had half as much to think about. See, this stewardess was a real strange one. First of all, she looked strange. Something about her hair . . . or her makeup. Her cheeks had a cakey look, and when she had put on her lipstick, she had drawn it above the natural line of her lips. Also, she painted on her eyelashes. You know, dark little lines painted on her eyelids. The whole effect was pretty weird. Even when you get a makeover at the Washington Mall, you don't come out looking *that* strange.

But worst of all, she was a total spacehead. Now most of the stewardesses I've met have been pretty down-to-earth. If you want a Coke, they give you a Coke. But this one I had to practically flag down anytime I wanted anything. The main trouble was, sitting next to me, in the aisle seat, was a very attractive guy. He was sandy-haired, good-looking, and had on a crisp white oxford shirt with the sleeves rolled up. Well, this stewardess practically drooled every time she walked by him.

"Can I get you anything, sir?" she asked.

When they came around with the beverage cart, he got an orange juice, and then she wheeled the cart right on! What about me?

"Excuse me," I said. "Excuse me."

"Excuse me," the man said. "This young girl didn't get a beverage."

"Oh, she didn't?" said the stewardess. She would've been blinking her eyelashes, only she couldn't. They were painted on.

"Tomato juice, please," I said. That was that.

Then she came around selling headsets for the music channels and the movie. Once again, the stewardess sold one to Mr. Handsome and ignored me. Once again, Mr. Handsome came to my rescue. When I finally got my headset, he winked at me.

"Now you know why I always get an aisle seat," he said.

Mr. Handsome's name was actually Tom and he turned out to be not a bad seatmate at all. He was a theater director, he said, and he was flying out to California to audition some actors. Wow! I thought. A theater director! I couldn't wait to tell Stacey. He and I had a little conversation about *Paris Magic* (which I hadn't even *seen*, just heard about from Stacey), and he wrote down the names of some other shows he thought I might enjoy.

"Gee, thanks," I said.

I tucked the slip of paper into the pocket of my cotton traveling jacket.

Well, Mr. Handsome (I mean Tom) had some

scripts with him that he had to read, so I listened to the music on the headphones and paged through my book and magazines. But I was getting much too excited to do any real reading.

When it was time for lunch, Tom turned to me and said, "Do you think we'll have to go to battle for you again?" But lunch, I figured, would be no problem. I had ordered a vegetarian lunch ahead of time. You can do that on airlines if you don't want to eat the regular food they give you. I'm not a strict vegetarian, but the vegetarian meals on the planes are always much better.

Anyway, our stewardess had about half the plane to serve before she got to our row.

"Here you go," she smiled at Tom.

"And for the young lady?" he said.

"I get a vegetarian meal," I said.

"No you don't," she said flatly.

"Yes," I said. "I ordered it when I got my ticket."

"Name?" she asked briskly.

"Dawn Schafer."

The stewardess disappeared to the back of the plane and came back with a computer printout. She ran her finger down a list.

"Schafer, Schafer, Schafer . . . ," she said. "Oh. Here you are. Oh, dear."

"Is there a problem?" asked Tom.

"Well," said the stewardess. "I did have a meal for you, but I gave it away. To that gentleman three rows up. He asked for one and I thought it was his."

She handed me a tray with a regular meal. No apology. No question about whether or not I was a strict vegetarian. What if I *couldn't* eat meat?

"Oh, well," she said. "There's certainly no way we can get another meal *in flight*."

Tom was looking faintly amused. I peeled back the tinfoil of my airplane lunch. Ew! It looked like the Friday lunch at Stoneybrook Middle School. There was some kind of meat with some kind of sauce on it. Mystery meat, I thought, and there was some soppy cole slaw and this disgusting rubbery Jell-O with globby things inside. There was also a salad (okay, I could eat that). And there was a piece of cornbread that *did* look more edible than the rest. What a lunch — cornbread and salad. I turned the meat over with my fork and thought about how Kristy would react if this were really a cafeteria lunch.

"Ew," she'd probably say. "Fried monkey brains." (Or something even grosser.)

Tom offered me his cornbread to help fill me up.

The rest of the flight was, well . . . long. Think of it — how often do you have to sit in a cramped seat for six hours straight? The movie was a shoot-'em-up, which filled the time, but not much else.

The stewardess, though, had one last opportunity to bungle things. After lunch, when she came around with coffee and tea, I asked if I could have a little real milk to put in my tea. (All she had on the tray was packets of that white chemical stuff.)

"Sure thing," she smiled, with that too-red smile of hers.

Minutes passed, many minutes, and again I had to flag her down.

"My milk, please?" I said.

"Oh, right."

She disappeared, came back, and tossed two of the chemical packets on my tray.

"There you go," she said, and she was gone.

"Do you get the feeling we're characters in some play?" Tom smiled. "A comedy?"

But, really, what did I care about "coffee whitener" or mystery meat or even irritating stewardesses? When the flight was over, I'd never see her again. When the flight was over, I'd be landing in my favorite place in the whole world . . . California!

The pilot's voice came over the intercom.

"We're preparing to land at the John Wayne/ Orange County Airport," he said. (That's really what the airport's called. Honest.)

The wheels of the plane hit the runway, I felt the power of the plane pulling back, and there I was!

When I walked off the plane and into the waiting room, my heart was pounding. There were Dad and Jeff on the other side of the guide rope, waiting and waving, both of them with big, gigundo smiles. Behind Jeff another face squeezed through. Sunny! When I got through the crowd, Jeff took my carry-on, and Dad grabbed me up and swung me around.

"Sunshine!" he said.

"Oh, Daddy," I blushed. (I would have to tell him not to call me Sunshine when Sunny was around. It wasn't just embarrassing, it'd be *confusing*.)

While we waited for my suitcase, everyone chattered at once. I told them all about the stewardess. Jeff told me about all the fun they had planned. Dad kept beaming and ruffling my hair. He even started snapping his fingers and singing that old song, "California Girls." He sure was acting goony.

"That's what fathers are for," he laughed.

It hit me how much I'd missed him.

Before we left, we picked up some postcards of the big John Wayne statue that towers over the airport. (I was now in California, all right.) In the car on the way home, Sunny grinned at me and hinted that she had something to tell me.

"It's sort of a surprise," she said, but she wouldn't tell me any more than that. "Just come over to my house tomorrow night," she said. "Five o'clock."

Sunny always did love surprises. It sounded pretty mysterious to me. I wondered what she had up her sleeve.

CHAPTER 4

Dear Dawn,

I'm writing this before you leave so you get it when you arrive. And anyway, I miss you already. As you read this, you're probably getting ready to go to the beach or to Disneyland, or you're probably lunching with movie stars. (Do they have movie stars in Anaheim?) Are the boys cute? Is everyone tan? Write me back!

Your (best) friend,
Mary Anne

When I woke up that Monday, my first morning back in California, at first I wasn't sure where I was. The sun was streaming in through the flowered curtains — the same curtains I had had when I lived here before. Maybe I had never left? From down the hall I heard silverware clinking and I also smelled something wonderful. Breakfast! I threw on my bathrobe and padded down the long, cool, tiled hall to the kitchen. There was Mrs. Bruen, the housekeeper Dad had hired. I'd never met her before, but we introduced ourselves.

Mrs. Bruen was busy organizing breakfast, so I sat at the table and took in the room. Everything seemed so spacious to me, compared to our little house in Connecticut. The rooms were so big, and the windows . . . Everything was wide open.

Our California house really is cool. It's all on one floor, but that one floor is long and wide and snakes around on two sides. The house is really shaped like a square, with only the top side missing. The floors are all tiled with terra cotta and there are slanted skylights in almost all the rooms. Now that Mrs. Bruen was taking care of it, the place was bright and sparkling.

Pretty soon Dad and Jeff stumbled into the kitchen. I'd forgotten that I'd be up earlier than they would, with the time change and all. Since it was Monday, usually Dad would be going to work, but he'd arranged to take off the first week of my visit, and that day he was taking Jeff and me . . . to Disneyland!

"All riiight!" said Jeff.

Jeff and I have been to Disneyland lots of times before, since it's right in Anaheim and that's near where our house is, but believe me, Disneyland is always a treat.

Mrs. Bruen brought our breakfast over to the table. She'd made fresh melon slices, cheese-and-egg puffs, fresh-squeezed orange juice, and wheat crisps. Yum!

"Beats a bowl of dry granola," I said, thinking of my last meal in Connecticut. My mouth was full.

"What?" asked Dad.

"Not important," I smiled.

"So what do you kids want to see today at Disneyland?" Dad asked. "It'd be nice to have some idea before we hit those lines and crowds."

That's Dad. Mr. Organization.

"Star Tours!" cried Jeff. "Big Thunder Mountain Railroad! Jungle Cruise! Space Mountain!" He kept going. "Matterhorn! Pirates of the Caribbean! Davy Crockett's Explorer Canoes! Penny Arcade!"

"Whoa! Slow down," laughed Dad.

Disneyland is made up of seven theme areas, and Jeff had managed to name exhibits and rides in every single one. Dad grabbed a pad and a pen.

"I knew it would be a good idea to talk about this beforehand," he said. "Okay, let's narrow down what areas of the park we're going to."

Jeff named three choices (Tomorrowland, Bear Country, and Frontierland) and I named mine (Fantasyland, New Orleans Square, and Jungleland). You'll notice that none of our choices overlapped.

"Of course you don't agree," said Dad. "That would be too easy. How about if you each pick two? We could probably manage to squeeze in four altogether."

"Does that count Main Street?" I asked. (Main Street, U.S.A., is the area leading into the park.)

"I guess not," Dad smiled. "Four, plus Main Street."

"All riiight!" Jeff said loudly. Jeff was already starting to get what Dad calls "Disneyland Wild."

"So what'll it be?" Dad asked. "Two each."

"Tomorrowland and Frontierland!" said Jeff. "No, Tomorrowland and Bear Country! No! I mean, Tomorrowland and Frontierland! Yeah, that's my vote."

My choices were Fantasyland and New Orleans Square.

Then Dad asked us what rides we wanted to go on and what things we wanted see. By the time we got out of the house and on the freeway, we had the whole trip planned out.

Disneyland is really super. I'd forgotten how much I love it. Dad bought our "Passports" at the front gate. Those are the tickets that let you go all through the park and on all the rides. (Of course, you can't buy things, like food or souvenirs, with them, but I'd brought along plenty of baby-sitting money for extras.) Jeff had brought his camera with him and took my picture by the Mickey Mouse face as we walked in.

"Dawn! Dawn! Stand over here!" he called to me.

It's things like that that let me know just how much Jeff really likes me. That was only the first picture of many. He must've taken two whole rolls of me that day.

We entered the park and walked up Main Street, U.S.A., which is made up to look like a small American town at the turn of the last century. It has horse-drawn streetcars and an old-fashioned fire engine, and because our visit was in the spring, there were tulips blooming everywhere. All the shops that line the street look like old shops, but you can buy really cool things in them.

I dragged Dad and Jeff into three stores. One for postcards (I was going to have a lot of *those* to write), one for Mickey Mouse ears (I bought a pair for each member of the Baby-sitters Club), and in the last store I got a special present just for Mary Anne (a plush Minnie Mouse doll for her bed).

"What do you say, think we've had enough?" teased Dad.

"No!" cried Jeff.

We had just begun.

At the end of Main Street is Sleeping Beauty's Castle, and that's the entrance to Fantasyland. When I was a little kid, I thought that castle was the most beautiful thing I'd ever seen. I could picture myself moving right into it. It really is fantastic. When I walk over the moat and through the castle, I really feel like I'm in Disneyland.

In Fantasyland, Jeff and I went on the Mad Tea Party ride (you sit inside these oversized teacups and spin all around) and on the Matterhorn Bobsleds. (Dad let Jeff pick one roller coaster ride and that one was it.)

From there we went on to Tomorrowland (with Jeff running ahead all the way). Of course, Jeff wanted to go on Star Tours, which has a really cool flight simulator.

"Too bad, Dawn," Jeff teased as we waited in line. " 'Children under three not allowed.' "

Believe it or not, that's exactly the kind of talk you miss when you don't have a brother around. They drive you crazy, but I have to admit, they can be pretty funny.

"Onward!" said Dad, once we left Star Tours.

We caught the train that circles the park and rode it all the way to Frontierland. That's where Jeff wanted to go on the Mark Twain Steamboat. "Ah, here we go," said Dad. "A ride for old fogies like me."

The steamboat circles an island and I like to pretend that I'm Mark Twain, navigating the Mississippi, thinking up the stories I'm going to write.

"So. We're finished," Dad said as we got off the boat. "We've done everything on our list."

There was a teasing twinkle in his eye.

"No way!" cried Jeff. "You forgot New Orleans Square!"

Jeff was still more than a little "Disneyland Wild."

Everybody was getting hungry, so we decided to stop in one of the New Orleans "buffeterias" . . . after one more ride.

"Pirates of the Caribbean!" shouted Jeff.

"No," I said. "Haunted Mansion. That was my whole reason for picking New Orleans Square."

"You could split up," Dad suggested.

That's exactly what we did.

Haunted Mansion is right up my (spooky, ghost-ridden) alley. On the outside it's an old New Orleans house. You know the kind. It has those wrought-iron, curlicue trellises bordering all the porches. Inside, though, it's a real spook house. To go through, you get in a Doom Buggy. Sound creepy? That's the least of it. Ghost Shadows are cast on all the walls, and eerie music plays in the background. Upstairs, in the attic, there's about an *inch* of dust on everything. I'm telling you, one trip through Haunted Mansion equals about *ten* good ghost stories. And I ought to know.

Jeff and I met Dad at the French Market restaurant, where he had already snared a table for us.

"Yum!" I said, as I looked at the menu. It was hard to decide between Cajun-seasoned trout or spinach quiche.

"Want to split them?" Dad asked. It was the perfect solution.

Now that we were sitting down and eating, Jeff began to wind down. Well, a little bit. We finished our meals and watched the Mark Twain steamboat glide by beyond the restaurant porch.

"Hey, Dawn," Jeff said. "Watch this."

Jeff made one of his silly monkey faces.

"Glad to see your sister, huh?" Dad laughed.

"Yeah," Jeff said sheepishly. He smiled at me, an awkward, self-conscious smile. "Sometimes I miss you, Dawn," he said.

Dad ruffled my hair, as if I were a puppy or something.

"We *both* miss you," he said. "That much is for sure."

There I was, back in Disneyland, sitting with my dad and my brother, and both of them being gushy. It sure felt good.

Dad looked at his watch.

"What time do you have to be at Sunny's, Dawn?" he asked.

"Five o'clock," I said. Whatever her surprise was, I'd better be on time.

"I think we have time to do one last thing," said Dad.

"Jungle Cruise!" shouted Jeff. He was never at a loss for ideas.

"No, this one's for your old man," said Dad. "I spotted it right as we came in the park. Back to Main Street, guys. Let's go."

"Where are we going?" asked Jeff.

"You'll see," said Dad.

He had that glint in his eye.

When we got back to Main Street, Dad led us straight to the Main Street Cinema, an old movie house that plays old cartoon classics, ones like *Steamboat Willie* and *Mickey's Polo Team*. It was really fun to see them.

"They sure don't look much like the cartoons we have today," I said.

"They're better," said Dad.

"No way!" said Jeff.

All in all, it had been a perfect day in Disneyland. And the day wasn't over yet, either. I couldn't wait to get home to see Sunny. I couldn't imagine what she might have for a surprise.

CHAPTER 5

Monday

Dear Everybody,

Well, I just cam't seem to get baby-
sitting off the brain. I'm mailing this to
Claudia's so you can all read it at your
meeting and I've just come from a meeting
of my own. No kidding! There's a California
branch of the Baby-sitters Club. It's called
the We ♥ Kids Club and my friend Sunny
started it. Some of the things about the
club are the same, but it's *very* California.
I'll tell all when I return.

Love,
Dawn

No wonder Sunny wanted to surprise me. When
I got back from Disneyland, I ran over to her

house. (She lives only a few houses down the block. I used to be there so often I could find it in my sleep.) I got there at five o'clock on the dot. Sunny's mom opened the door.

"Dawn," she smiled. "Look at you! Look how you've grown! Oh, I know I'm not supposed to say that. Come in. Come in."

Sunny clambered down the stairs. She was grinning from ear to ear. She had a bandana in her hands. Sunny and her surprises . . .

"Hold still," she said to me, "and close your eyes."

She tied the bandana on me like a blindfold.

"What . . . ?" I said.

"I told you," she insisted. "It's a *surprise*!"

Sunny took my arm and led me up the stairs to her room. She swung open the door and undid my blindfold.

"Ta-da!" she said.

There, in the room, sat two other girls, Maggie Blume and Jill Henderson. I remembered them because I used to be in their class at school. Was this the surprise? I smiled faintly. I knew these girls, but I hadn't ever really been great friends with them.

"Sit down," said Sunny. "Make yourself at

home. What are you waiting for? Haven't you ever been to a meeting of a baby-sitters club before?"

Sunny still had that wide, teasing grin stretched across her face.

"Baby-sitting club?" I said.

"Yup," said Sunny, proudly, "the We ♥ Kids Club." And she told me all about it.

"Remember all those letters you sent me?" asked Sunny. "With all the news about your club?"

"Sure," I said. (I must've sent her about a hundred.)

"Well," she said. "It sounded like a good idea. I'd been baby-sitting a lot around the neighborhood, and so had Maggie and Jill —"

"It sounded like a *great* idea," Jill broke in. "Before, we were all sitting, but we were just out there on our own."

"So we got together the club," said Maggie.

"And we named it the We ♥ Kids Club," said Jill.

"And it was all I could do to keep it a secret!" Sunny laughed.

To tell you the truth, I was shocked she'd been able to carry it off. Well, if there was a surprise involved, Sunny could do almost anything.

"How long have you been meeting?" I asked.

"Six months," Sunny grinned. "Six long, *silent* months."

Of course, I had lots of questions. I wanted to know exactly how they ran their club. Some things were the same as ours — Sunny had gotten a lot of ideas from my letters.

"Like advertising," she said. "When we first started, we made up flyers and stuck them in every mailbox for ten blocks."

"And of course we collect dues," said Jill.

"For Kid-Kits!" Sunny cried out. She was practically exploding from the excitement of finally getting to tell her secret.

"You have Kid-Kits, too?" I asked.

Kid-Kits are a great idea that Kristy thought up. They're boxes that we fill with all kinds of things for kids to play with — books, games, crayons, puzzles. We bring them to the houses we baby-sit at and, of course, the kids just love them. They're also good for business. They show we really are concerned and involved sitters.

Sunny pulled out her own Kid-Kit, and I took a look through. Play-Doh, cookie cutters, watercolors . . . and a cookbook!

" '*Kids Can Cook . . . Naturally,*' " I read.

"It's a great book," said Sunny. "All the recipes are easy for kids — none of them involve the oven or stove. And they all use natural foods."

"Wow," I said. Imagine if I tried to introduce that book to my club.

"Oh, yeah," said Sunny, "and we've got an appointment book."

She pulled out a thin notebook and opened it to the day's page.

Well, it certainly did look as if the clubs were a lot the same, but believe me, there were lots of differences, too.

After Sunny had told me about the club, I figured she would call the meeting to order. I almost expected her to pull out a director's chair, just like Kristy sits in, and call for order. Instead we just sort of sat around and talked some more. They told me all about Mr. Roberts, their science teacher, and asked me if Connecticut schools make you dissect a worm.

Then the phone rang. Maggie reached for it and took the call. She put her hand over the receiver and said, "Mrs. Peters. Thursday. Anybody take it?"

"I will," said Jill.

It was as simple as that.

"Don't you take the information and call them back?" I asked. That's the way we did it.

"Why?" said Maggie.

I just shrugged my shoulders. Somehow it seemed too complicated to explain.

After the call, Sunny wandered off to the kitchen and brought us back a snack — apple slices with natural peanut butter.

It's true, I thought. I really am back in California. This was a far cry from Claudia's Ring Dings.

"So who are your officers?" I asked.

"Officers?" asked Sunny.

"You know, president, vice-president, secretary . . ."

"We don't have anything like that," said Sunny. "Everybody just does what they do."

"Oh," I said.

Another call came in. This time Sunny took the job.

Jill pulled a bottle of nail polish out of her purse and started working on her nails. I could just see Kristy if one of us tried that back in Stoneybrook.

I got up and looked at Sunny's bookshelves — two whole shelves of ghost stories. Sunny and I had fallen in love with ghost stories back in fourth grade, at just about the same time. When our class went to the school library, we used to race each other because we both wanted to get there first, to get whatever ghost books were in that week. (I can still hear Mrs. Wright, our teacher, now. "Girls! No running in the halls!") Sunny had a lot of new books on her shelves now, a lot of books I hadn't ever heard of, like *Ghost in Whitcomb's Briar* and *Seven Gothic Ghosts.*

"Have you read *Spirits, Spooks, and Ghostly Tales?"* asked Maggie.

"Maggie loves ghost stories, too," Sunny explained. "I got her into them."

"Phew, I have to sit down," I said. What had happened? Had I died and gone to Dawn heaven? It sure felt like it. I was in California, where the weather was warm and beautiful. I was staying with my wonderful, goofy dad and I had my good ol' brother back, too. Next, I found out my best friend in California had started up a baby-sitting club. Where they served *apple slices* for snacks. And to top it off, my old friends liked ghost stories, too! Sunny was piling up books in my arms to take back to Dad's with me.

"Vacation reading," she said.

Just then, the third and last call came in. It was Mrs. Austin, Dad's next-door neighbor. She needed someone Saturday during the day to sit for Clover and Daffodil. I'd been their sitter many times before when I'd lived in California.

"You want it?" Sunny smiled at me.

"You bet!" I said.

Jill handed me the notebook and I penciled myself in.

We still had a few minutes of the meeting to go, so Jill painted all our fingernails and we sat around, waving our hands back and forth to dry the shimmering gloss.

"I've got one more surprise for you," said Sunny, blowing on her nails.

Another surprise? Sunny's eyes were twinkling. She blurted out the news.

"Our school's on spring break these two weeks, too!"

"Perfect!" I squealed. It was.

When it was time to go home, I grabbed my stack of books, popped in to say good-bye to Sunny's mom, and practically skipped the whole way home. It was 5:30, but the sun was still bright. It warmed my shoulders and toasted my hair.

The We ♥ Kids Club might not be as busy or have as big a business as the Baby-sitters Club, but it sure was fun. I loved the way everything in

California was so easy, so free. I swung my hair from side to side as I skipped into the house.

"Hey," said Dad. "You look happy. Anything special?"

I stumbled to the table and dropped my books all over its top.

"Everything!" I laughed.

Dear Dawn,

Having a wonderful time. Wish you were here. Wait! That's what you're supposed to write to <u>us</u>. Actually, we do wish you were here. We sure could've used you the other night at the Newtons. The two of us sat for the Newtons, the Feldmans, <u>and</u> the Perkinses. That's eight kids! (Count 'em.) We figured out a game plan ahead of time — we were going to get the kids <u>out</u> of the house — but guess what? It rained. Help! But rain wasn't the only surprise. Tell you all about it when we see you.

Bye,
Mary Anne and Claudia

The Newtons, the Feldmans and the Perkinses. That's one big group, all right. And that group is a handful and a half.

Mrs. Newton had cleared everything ahead of time with Mary Anne and Claudia. All the parents were going out together for dinner and a concert, so it seemed natural to put the kids all together and get two sitters. The plan was that everyone would stay at the Newtons. Jamie Newton is four and his little sister Lucy is just a baby. They're real cute kids. By themselves they're a pleasure. Then there're the Perkins girls, Myriah, who's five and a half, Gabbie, who's two and a half, and Laura, the baby. (I hope you're counting babies. That makes *two*.) Baby-sitting for Myriah and Gabbie is usually as easy as baby-sitting for Jamie. Myriah's really smart and Gabbie is really cute. She calls everybody by their full names. "Hello, Dawn Schafer," she always says to me.

So far, so good. But when you put those kids together with the Feldmans, well, then you might have yourself a problem. The Feldman kids are Jamie and Lucy's cousins. There's Rob Feldman (he's ten), Brenda Feldman (she's six), and Rosie Feldman (she's four). Hmm, what can I say about the Feldmans? Well, to start, Rob is a girl-hater. He's got it in his head that girls are no good, and that goes double for girl baby-sitters. His sister Brenda is just a grouch. It's hard to get her to enjoy anything. And the little one, Rosie, well, she's a one-girl noise machine. (But the thing is, unlike a machine, you can't just turn her off. And she can really give a baby-sitter a headache.)

When I got to talk to Mary Anne about it, she told me that she and Claudia had tried to plan the whole thing out ahead of time. They were going to give the kids an early dinner, and then, while it was still light, they were going to put the babies in their carriages and march the whole group over to the school playground. Outside, Rosie could make as much noise as she wanted. Rob could even hate girls. He could show off on the monkey bars and feel as superior as he wanted. The other kids, of course, would be perfectly happy on the swing set or in the sandbox. And when they'd tired themselves out? Home to the Newtons' house and into pajamas.

Well, it sounded like a good plan. Mary Anne and Claudia were very pleased with themselves for having so much foresight. Except, of course, it rained. Early that evening, when the two of them arrived at the Newtons, the sky had turned a dark shade of purple and a few big, splotchy raindrops had already splattered the front walk.

Mary Anne looked at Claudia. Claudia looked at Mary Anne. Jamie answered the door.

"Hi-hi!" he said.

Gabbie was right behind.

"Hello, Mary Anne Spier. Hello, Claudia Kishi," she said.

Jamie and Gabbie, both with their characteristic welcomes. Mrs. Newton was right behind.

"Hi, girls. Great. You're a few minutes early. Everybody's here. The kids are in the playroom. I made a big pot of chili for dinner. The babies, of course, get their own food. Come in the kitchen, let me show you."

Mrs. Newton had organized everything as well as she could. Dinner was on the stove, cots and sleeping bags had been set out in the living room (this was going to be a *long* evening), and she had settled the kids in the playroom with coloring books and toys. (Rob was watching television.)

Mary Anne and Claudia went to the playroom and sat themselves among the group. Mrs. Perkins was there with the babies, who were playing on the floor with plush toys.

"They'll go to bed by seven, seven-thirty," she said.

The parents all gathered around their broods to say good-bye, then they were off. The crowd looked smaller after the six adults had left but, somehow, it did not look quite small enough. Big drops of rain were now pelting the windows. (It kept up the whole night long.)

"How about one of us takes the babies, and the other the kids?" Claudia suggested.

Two little babies or six growing (active) kids. Somehow, it didn't seem balanced. Mary Anne looked skeptical.

"Okay, how 'bout we do it that way, then trade off?" Claudia suggested.

Mary Anne took baby duty first and Claudia took the kids.

Now, when you're baby-sitting for a crew, you'd better place yourself so that you can keep an eye on everybody at the same time. That's one thing we learned when we ran a play group last summer. You can't afford to get so involved with any one kid that the whole group falls apart. Claudia pulled a chair up to the play table. Jamie and Gabbie were working at one end and Myriah, Brenda, and Rosie were working at the other. All the kids had fresh sheets of white paper and their own little box of crayons. (Thank you, Mrs. Newton.) Except for Rob's television blaring in the background, the room was surprisingly peaceful.

Brenda pressed hard on her crayon to color in the giraffe she was drawing. *Snap!* It broke in half.

"My brown!" she said. "My brown broke!"

She grabbed the brown crayon out of her sister's box.

"Gimme!" Rosie shouted back.

"It's mine!" shouted Brenda.

Rosie began banging on the table. She had probably been waiting for just such an opportunity to make a lot of noise.

Now, Claudia is really the only sitter who has a lot of experience with the Feldman kids. A lot of experience, in this case, really means only two times. The first time she encountered this kind of problem, she ignored it and, when they didn't get any attention, the Feldman kids calmed down. The second time she sat for them, Kristy was along. Kristy had let out a sharp, shrill whistle and called the whole scene to a halt. Claudia didn't know how to whistle like Kristy, so she quietly took the brown crayon out of Brenda's hand and gave it back to Rosie.

"You know that's Rosie's crayon," she said gently.

Just then Mary Anne stepped in and took Brenda's hand. That's baby-sitting teamwork. "I need some help with the babies," she said. "Brenda, you're a good helper. You come over and work with me."

Surprisingly, Brenda got up from the table and

went to join Mary Anne. Claudia quieted Rosie and got her interested again in her picture. Rob looked over from the sidelines.

"I'm the oldest," he muttered. "And I know most about babies."

Mary Anne looked at him curiously.

"Would you like to join us, too?" she asked.

Rob eyed the babies.

"I'm watching television," he said. He turned his attention back to the screen.

Mary Anne and Brenda started a little rolling game for the babies with a cloth ball, but when Brenda rolled it, the ball rolled over toward Rob and bumped his knee.

"Here you go, babies," he said. He rolled the ball gently back.

Mary Anne shot Claudia a look as if to say, "Did you just see what I saw? Is that really Rob Feldman, girl-hater, sitting over there?"

Claudia shrugged her shoulders in reply. Maybe Rob didn't consider babies to be girls yet. Or maybe he had just grown out of his nasty phase. (After all, it had been almost a full year since Claudia had sat for him.)

"Blast off!" he said suddenly, his eyes fixed on the screen. "Babies into space!" Since he was watching a cowboy movie, no one knew quite what he meant.

The kids colored for awhile. At one point, Rosie started up her noise, banging her fists on the table, her feet on the floor, and loudly chanting a song she knew, but she was silenced by, of all people, Gabbie. When Rosie started her tirade, Gabbie put her hands over her ears and stared Rosie straight in the eye.

"You be quiet, Rosie Feldman," she said, very precisely. "You are really hurting my ears."

Rosie was so surprised at getting a reprimand from Gabbie that she screwed up her face and went back to her picture.

When it was time for dinner, Mary Anne volunteered to take Brenda and Myriah (the two oldest girls) to the kitchen to serve up the plates.

"What about the babies?" Claudia asked.

"Hmmm," said Mary Anne. "Maybe I could take them up and get them set up in their high chairs and the girls could serve the chili."

Rob swung around from the television.

"Little babies can't coordinate their hands with their eyes," he said. Then he looked at his cousin. "But you can, can't you, Lucy?"

Mary Anne shot Claudia another look. Well, it was worth a try, she thought.

"Rob," she asked, "why don't you come help me with the babies in the kitchen. Can you carry Lucy?"

Rob picked Lucy up and followed Mary Anne and the kitchen crew out of the playroom. He set Lucy into her high chair and strapped her in.

"How do you know so much about babies?" Mary Anne asked as she set the other baby down.

"Babies in Space," Rob said tersely.

"Is that a TV show?" Mary Anne asked.

"No," he said, as if everyone knew. "A book."

"Oh," said Mary Anne.

As it turned out, the book was a science fiction story about some scientists who send babies in a rocket to another planet. First, of course, they have to know everything about babies that they can, so the book is filled with little bits and snatches of scientific information about babies and how they develop.

Mary Anne opened a jar of strained pears, stuck a spoon in it, and set it down on Lucy's high-chair tray. Rob picked up the jar and started to feed her.

"When babies are nursing, they get immunities from their mothers," he said. He spooned some of the strained pear and aimed it high at Lucy's little mouth. "Ready! Aim! Fire!" He made rocket noises as he dipped the spoon into Lucy's waiting mouth.

Mary Anne told me later that she thought, Well, you just never know. Rob Feldman, girl-hater/baby-lover. Now he seemed more like future baby-sitter material. Who could figure it? Baby-sitting is always a surprise.

Dinner went fairly smoothly. Claudia maneuvered the seating so Brenda wasn't sitting next to Rosie. (Those two were just a *bad* combination.) And after dinner, Rob helped Claudia get the babies off to bed.

When the parents got home, all the kids were in their pajamas and *most* were asleep. (Brenda kept waking up confused. "Where am I?") The Perkinses and the Feldmans picked up their pajama-ed and sleepy-eyed kids, covered them with raincoats, and ran them out to their cars.

"Oh," said Mrs. Newton, as she shook out her umbrella. "What a refreshing evening. And how did it go for you girls?"

Mary Anne grinned at Claudia.

"*Surprisingly* well," said Mary Anne.

Thursday

Dear Kristy,

   As I'm writing this I'm wiggling my
toes in the hot sand and I just finished
slathering sun lotion all over my legs.
Oops! Got some on the postcard. Too bad
this isn't a letter. I'd stick some sand in
the envelope for you. As you can see, I'm
happy as a sand crab.

                        See you (too!) soon,
                                Dawn

Well, Thursday was what I would call a perfect
day. (Perfect except for the strange feelings that
were brewing inside me.) Dad volunteered to
take me and Jeff, plus the members of the We ♥
Kids Club, *plus* a friend of Jeff's . . . to the beach!

(Brave Dad.) Everyone gathered at our house after breakfast in the morning, and it did take us awhile to get going.

I had to run back into the house to slip a cover-up over my bikini so I'd feel okay for the car ride. (What if we stopped at a store for drinks or something?) Sunny, Jill, and Maggie arrived in their bikinis and the sight was just too much for Jeff and his friend Luke. "Underwear!" they screamed. "The girls are going to the beach in their *underwear!*" (Ten-year-old boys will be ten-year-old boys, all right.)

There we were, all dragging beach totes with suntan lotion and beach towels, and all wearing flip-flops. No question about where we were headed. I took a look at us as we gathered in the driveway and noticed that we were all blond. Jeff and I are white-blond, but everyone there was some kind of blond or other. Well, this really was a stereotypical California group.

We waited for Jeff to run back into the house (two times) for more comic books, I checked to see that I had stuck my Walkman in my bag and, finally, we were off.

In the car, Jeff and Luke insisted on singing "99 Bottles of Beer on the Wall."

"Dad," I said. "Make them stop."

"I think it would take a power greater than I," he said.

Luckily, the boys got bored after about 82 bottles.

When we got to the beach it really was not very crowded. People in California wait until it's really summer to go to the beach, and also, it was the middle of the week. Actually, it was beautiful beach weather. Not a cloud in that whole wide blue sky, and the sun was beating down, warming the sand, the ocean, and us!

I ran ahead and found us a big stretch of sand. (We *needed* a big space.) "Blonds over here!" I shouted and everyone ran to the spot and spread out their towels.

"You're right about blonds," said Dad. "We look like the Swedish delegation to the blond convention."

And the whole rest of the day, that's what he called us, "The Blond Convention." Of course, it didn't help when Jill and Maggie pulled out their Sun-Light and combed it through their hair.

"Blond and want to be blonder?" Dad teased. He was using a deep, announcer's voice, like a TV commercial. "Try our products. That's Products for Blonds. In the pale yellow packaging."

We arranged the beach towels so that Dad was on one side of me, and Sunny and the girls were on the other. Jeff and Luke spread their towels a little ways away. I think they were looking for a place that would give them the best aim — at us — because, as we lay there in the sun, all slathered up, Jeff and Luke tossed little bits of dried seaweed and tiny pieces of shells onto our oiled backs and bellies.

"Bull's-eye!" Jeff yelled, when he got a shell right on Dad's bellybutton.

"Why don't you guys take a shell hike?" Dad suggested. He handed them the red plastic beach pail we had brought along.

"BO-RING," said Jeff.

"How about digging for clams?" Dad suggested.

"Yeah!" said Luke and Jeff at the same time. They were off and running.

Sunny, Maggie, and Jill decided to head down to the edge of the ocean and wade in. I wasn't really warm enough yet, so I decided to stay put and let the sun do its work.

"So here you are, Sunshine," Dad said when we found ourselves alone. "Sunshine in the sunshine."

Dad can be a real cornball sometimes. He grinned at me, then squinted out at the ocean.

"I'm glad you could come for a visit," he said.

"Me too."

Somebody walked by us with a radio. I could tell Dad was going to start up a serious talk, and I wasn't sure if I was ready for it. Well, ready or not, a father-daughter chat was in the air. I waited for Dad to start.

"So how's it going in Connecticut?" he asked.

"It's okay," I said.

"School?"

"Fine."

"Friends?"

"Friends? Friends are great," I said. I sat up on my towel and started to push my fingers through the sand.

"How does Jeff seem to you?" Dad continued.

Jeff seemed fine, and I told Dad so. I told him again how unhappy Jeff had been in Connecticut and how much trouble he'd gotten into at school and all.

"I guess Jeff's the type who just needs to be home in California," Dad mused.

"Lucky him," I said, half under my breath. I was surprised at how sullen I sounded all of a sudden. Usually I'm about as even-tempered as they come.

Dad glanced at me and then stared out at the surf where my friends were playing.

"So how's your mother?" Dad asked after awhile.

"Oh, you know Mom," I said. "I have to check her every time she goes out of the house for —" I almost said, "for a date with the Trip-Man," but I caught myself just in time. I really didn't want to get into a discussion about the Trip-Man with Dad. I paused awkwardly, then said quickly, "— for work. Out of the house for work."

It felt silly to have something I couldn't talk to Dad about. Somehow, the whole conversation was feeling awkward to me. I didn't know what was the matter. I dug my fingers deeper into the sand.

"Is she, uh . . . doing okay?" Dad asked.

"Pretty good," I said. The truth was, Mom *was* doing okay. She might be scattered, but that was just Mom. She might be a little weepy every now and then, but that was natural — her family had been split up. "She likes Connecticut," I said. "She sees Granny and Pop-Pop. She loves the farmhouse. . . ."

"I hear you have a secret passageway," Dad smiled. "Something right out of one of your ghost stories, huh?"

I told him all about the passageway, about how we had found it, and how Mallory's brother Nicky had discovered it before any of us.

"He still hides out in there sometimes," I said. "Sometimes when he just needs some solitude."

"In a family with eight kids?" Dad said. "I can see why."

"Well," I said glumly, "I don't have that problem." Again, the tone of my voice surprised me. What was the matter with me? I was in California, at the beach. . . . The *last* thing I should have been doing was complaining.

Dad knew right away that something was up. He waited awhile before he said anything. Dad's good that way. He gives you whatever time you need to think things through.

"A little lonely, are you?" he said.

I hadn't thought of it that way before, exactly. Maybe I was. I wasn't sure what I was feeling.

Just then Jeff and Luke ran up and dropped a little sand crab in my lap.

"Ew!" I screamed.

"Jeff. Luke," Dad said sternly.

All of a sudden I felt like running, moving, getting up, doing something. I popped up, brushed the sand crab back onto the sand, and took off for the ocean. Sunny and the others were now waist-deep in the water.

"Aughhh!" I cried as I ran toward them, into the surf. The water was cold and shocked my skin, but I plunged in, ducked under, and came up wet and dripping. I bounded out to where my friends stood. The waves crashed against us and we jumped them and laughed. I waved to Dad back on shore. Suddenly I thought how happy, how *ecstatic*, I was to be home.

When my friends and I came back in, we were blue-lipped and shivering. Dad bundled us up in towels and we let the sun do the rest.

I sat at the edge of my towel and built a little sand castle.

"Want to help?" I asked my friends. They didn't.

I stuck some shells in the castle for turrets. My emotions were beginning to calm. I thought, in passing, of Claudia. The sand castle looked like something she might make. If Claudia were with us, I thought with a smile, she'd probably be building castles all up and down the shore.

After awhile we had a wonderful lunch that Mrs. Bruen had packed us — avocado salad with shrimp and sprouts and an unusual potato salad made with fresh parsley and herbs.

Yum! My friends and I gobbled it up.

When the sun started to fade, we gathered up our things and straggled back to the car.

"Blond Convention, ho!" Dad called, leading the way.

That night, much later, Dad suggested that I call Mom, just to say hi.

I wasn't sure, but I think she sounded a little shaky-voiced when she answered the phone.

"Dawn!" she said. Her voice was surprised. "So how are you?" she asked. "Are you having a good time?"

I babbled on about the beach, the weather, the housekeeper, my friends.

"We already went to Disneyland, then today we went to the beach. . . . And, Mom, I don't even have to miss the Baby-sitters Club. Saturday I baby-sit for Clover and Daffodil, and Sunny runs her club just like ours, except it's much more relaxed. . . . I'm having a *great* time. Jeff is real happy, and Dad is just super. . . ."

I think I must've babbled on for quite awhile. Out of nervousness? Something about it felt wrong.

"I'm so glad, honey," Mom said, when I had

finished. Jeff was calling me in the background, so I put Dad on the phone.

There we were in our busy, active household, a family, and there was Mom in the farmhouse all alone. I guess, at the time, I didn't think of it that way. I certainly didn't realize how much *I* was really missing Mom. I guess I wasn't sure *what* I was thinking.

CHAPTER 8

Saturday

Dear Claudia,

Sorry about that rain you and Mary Anne had when you baby-sat the other night. Here? It never rains. This afternoon I baby-sat for Clover and Daffodil — you remember I told you they're my old neighbors? Well, it was one of my all-time great baby-sitting days. Let me put it this way — I came home with a better tan than I started with. Ah, California. You know how I love the warm outdoors....

Dawn

My first job for the We ♥ Kids Club really was a great success. When I got to their house, Clover and Daffodil practically knocked each other over trying to say hello to me. Daffodil was a little more subdued — she's nine years old and more grown-up than Clover, who's only six. Clover was pulling at my sundress before I could even get through the door.

"Whoa!" I said. "It's only me."

"Dawn!" cried Clover. "My favorite baby-sitter in the whole wide world!"

I must admit, when one of the kids gives you a compliment like that, it's not very hard to love your job.

Mrs. Austin gave me a big hug hello. It was like I was a long-lost friend, returning from a great war or something.

"The kids have been so excited," she said. She drew me into the room.

I always loved the Austins' house, especially the living room. Mrs. Austin is a weaver. Dad said when they were young, she and her husband used to be "flower children." (I think he means hippies.) That's why Clover and Daffodil have such odd names. Now, though, Mrs. Austin weaves professionally for a few stores that carry expensive hand-crafted goods, and she has three different-sized looms in her living room. The looms sit on the polished wood floor underneath the big bay window. I love to take a look at what she's working on. She mostly makes pieces with deep, rich natural colors. Beautiful warm browns and earthy reds. And there's always something different on the looms.

"I never have to redecorate," she laughs. "Whenever I change projects, I change the whole visual effect of the room."

That day, Clover and Daffodil were each wearing hand-woven cotton vests that their mother had made for them. Clover pulled a small change purse out of her vest pocket and shook the money into her hand.

"Pieces of eight!" she cried. "I'm rich!"

I had forgotten about Clover's wild imagination.

"I gave each of the kids some money," Mrs. Austin explained. "There's a small carnival that's set up over in the field behind the mall. Since it's such a beautiful day, I thought you might want to walk the girls over and spend the afternoon there."

"Super," I said. The afternoon couldn't be shaping up better.

Mrs. Austin grabbed her shawl (hand-woven, of course) and headed out the door. She was going to a Craft Council meeting, so she'd be gone all afternoon.

Before we could go off to the fair, Clover and

Daffodil had to drag me all over the house and show me everything that was new. It *had* been a long time since we'd seen each other.

"This is the kitchen and this is the refrigerator," said Clover in her excitement.

"She knows *that*, silly," said Daffodil. "Come on. Let me show you my science project."

We went all through Clover's and Daffodil's rooms. They showed me new clothes, new toys, new books, new school projects, report cards, you name it.

As they were winding down, I sat on Clover's bed and she got out her comb to comb through my long hair. (She always did love to do that.)

"I think somebody spun your hair into gold," she said. "Did you ever meet a little guy named Rumpelstiltskin?"

Of course I told her no, but I think Clover secretly went on believing her own imaginative version. Daffodil sat quietly by. Sometimes, even though she's older, she gets overshadowed by Clover's more outgoing nature. She's also at that gangly stage — her legs and arms seem a little too long for her body.

"Well," I said, standing up. "Shall we head for the carnival?"

Clover popped up beside me. "To see the

Ferris wheel!" she cried. She was down the stairs and out the door, with Daffodil and I trailing behind her.

The day was warm and dry and the bright blue sky was streaked with thin, wispy clouds. We had only a short hike to get to the fairgrounds. Just as Mrs. Austin had said, the fair was set up behind the mall. There were a couple of rides — a ferris wheel and an octopus ride with cages that looped up and over.

"A space creature!" shouted Clover.

There were also lots of midway games, plenty of food booths (Hmmm. Hot dogs and cotton candy. Not my idea of a healthy treat), and a fenced-off ring with pony rides.

Clover had me by one hand and I had Daffodil by the other. Clover dragged us from one booth to the next, trying to decide where we should start.

"How about the ring toss?" Daffodil asked in a smallish voice.

"Ring toss!" Clover boomed in echo.

No sooner had she spotted it than we were there. The girls plunked down their money and got their handful of rings. As you can imagine, Clover was an enthusiastic player. Enthusiastic, but not very skilled. Out of six rings she got . . . six misses.

"Oh, well," she shrugged. It was Daffodil's turn.

Clover had pitched her rings quickly, but Daffodil took her time. She eyed the hook that was the target. She scrunched her eyebrows in concentration. One hit! Two! Three! A miss. Four hits! Another miss.

"Wow!" I said. "Four out of six. That's not bad at all."

Daffodil smiled shyly. Something about her reminded me of Shannon — she was like a puppy who had not yet grown into its paws.

"Can I try again?" she asked quietly.

"Sure," I said.

Daffodil bought another round of rings. Again she scrunched up her eyebrows in concentration before she started. One hit. Two. Three. Four. A miss. Another miss.

"Oh," I groaned. "So close!"

Daffodil smiled and said nothing. Clover was already dragging us over to the pony ring.

"Want to ride?" I asked Daffodil.

Daffodil emptied her change purse into her hand and counted her quarters.

"Nah," she said. "I think I'll wait."

Clover ran through the gate and hopped on the pony.

"Giddy-up!" she cried. She nudged the pony's

ribs with her heels, but the pony stood still. It was waiting for a command from the young woman in jeans and cowboy boots who would lead it around the ring.

"Yeehaw!" cried Clover.

I looked at Daffodil and grinned.

"Who do you think Clover thinks she is?" I asked.

"Annie Oakley, I betcha," said Daffodil.

As it turned out, Clover was thinking of herself more as a modern-day rodeo star. She explained that to us after the pony ride and before the ferris wheel. Then, after the ferris wheel, of course, she had to go on the octopus ride. When she was finished, we were all ready for a little refreshment.

"Cotton candy!" yelled Clover.

Well, what could I do? Clover bought her cotton candy, and Daffodil and I got some fruit juice and vegetable fritters. We found a patch of grass to sit on at the edge of the carnival and let the sights and sounds play around us as we ate our snack.

Daffodil counted her change again.

"I could play two more times," she said.

"Ring toss?" I asked.

She nodded her head. We waited for Clover to finish her cone of cotton candy (of course it got all over her face. She looked like some sort of sticky, pink elf), then we headed back to the booth. Daffodil looked determined. She may be a quiet one, I thought, but she's got a lot of resolve.

Her first game came in short of the others. Only three hits and three misses. Daffodil licked her lips as she bought the rings for her fourth and last game. One hit! Two! Three! Four! Five! . . . We all held our breath. . . . Six!

"Yippee!" yelled Clover. She jumped up and down and shook her sister by the arm.

Daffodil's face broke into a wide, bright smile. "I knew it," she said. "I knew I could do it."

In the back of the booth was a shelf of stuffed animals, which were the prizes.

"The pink elephant, please," Daffodil said to the man running the booth.

It certainly was pink. It was as pink as the cotton candy that still stuck to Clover's cheeks.

"Come on," I said. "Let's go home while we're winners. And let's get you cleaned up." I ruffled Clover's hair. "Even rodeo stars need to look good for their parents."

When Mrs. Austin got home, she had the same reaction I did to the stuffed elephant.

"It certainly is pink," she laughed. "Congratulations, sweetie."

I don't think Mrs. Austin was going to pick that color for her next weaving project.

The day had been so pleasant, so easy. I was thinking how I couldn't wait to tell Sunny and the others all about it. There was a knock on the door. It was Jeff.

"Mom's on the phone," he said. "Come on."

Mrs. Austin slipped me my pay and I ran home after Jeff.

"Bye, Dawn-Best-Baby-sitter," Clover called after me.

As I was running I found myself thinking not of Mom, but of the day, of Clover and Daffodil, of Mrs. Austin, the We ♥ Kids Club. . . . I got on the phone and Mom started right in talking. She told me about Granny and Pop-Pop and then she said she'd run into Kristy and her mother at the store. "Oh," she said, "and Mary Anne called."

Wow! Mom, Granny and Pop-Pop, Kristy, even Mary Anne. I hadn't thought of any of them all day long. What did that mean, I wondered. I suddenly felt wrenched out of one world and yanked into another.

CHAPTER 9

Dear Dawn,

Thought you might want to know that nothing has changed in Stoneybrook. Saturday I baby-sat at the Brewers, and you'll be interested to know that Ben Brewer, the old ghost, is alive and well and living on the third floor. At least that's what Karen says. Me, I think Sam has something to do with it. This time, anyway.

See ya,
Jessi

Well, some things never change. When you baby-sit for Karen Brewer, there's bound to be ghosts involved, or witches with magic spells, or some such spookiness. Jessi had taken a job at the Brewers' for Saturday afternoon. Kristy was going shopping with her mother, and Sam, Charlie, and Watson were out who knows where.

That left the younger ones — David Michael, Karen, and Andrew — in need of a sitter, so Jessi filled the job.

Kristy's mom walked Jessi around the house, giving her all the usual information — showing her where the emergency numbers were, the snacks, etc. Of course, Kristy followed right behind. Sometimes you'd think Kristy was the Baby-sitting Police, not just the president of our club.

"Aren't you going to ask about the first-aid kit?" she prompted Jessi.

"Uh, yeah," Jessi stumbled.

"It's right in the medicine cabinet," Kristy's mom said, smiling.

Mrs. Brewer could hardly get Kristy away from Jessi and out the door.

"Shannon and Boo-Boo have been fed," Kristy called from the doorway, "and the plants have been watered, and the dishwasher's run through."

"And the lawn has been mowed," Kristy's mom teased, "and the house has been painted, and the telephone bill's been paid."

Kristy blushed furiously.

"Okay, bye," she called to Jessi.

Jessi picked up Andrew and together they waved good-bye.

"Well," Jessi said, when the door had closed. "Now it's just the four of us."

"Oh, no," Karen said firmly. "Five. Ben Brewer."

"Right," Jessi smiled.

"Come on," Karen said, grabbing Jessi's hand. "Time to play Let's All Come In."

"Oh, no," groaned David Michael.

Let's All Come In is a favorite game of Karen's, if you can call it a game. She gets everyone to pretend that they're different characters in a hotel lobby, checking in. What it really is, is an excuse to play dress-up. Karen dresses up in a long black dress and a hat, and the boys wear sailor caps. I think David Michael has played this game one time too many.

"Andrew and I were in the middle of building a Lego city," he said. "Weren't we, Andrew?"

"Yup," Andrew agreed.

"Looks like it's just you and me," Karen said to Jessi.

"You, me, and Ben Brewer," Jessi smiled.

Jessi got the boys settled back in David Michael's bedroom, where there really was a Lego city in progress.

"I'm the architect," David Michael said importantly, "and Andrew is the construction boss. Right, Andrew?"

"Right," Andrew smiled. Construction boss sounded pretty good to him.

Karen took Jessi to her room and began to root through the trunk she kept her dress-up clothes in.

"Hmm," she said, looking Jessi up and down. "Do you want to be a cocktail waitress or do you want to be coming from the society ball?"

"Society ball, of course," Jessi replied.

"I don't think I have anything here to fit you," Karen said slowly. "You know what that means?"

"What?" asked Jessi.

"That means" — there was an ominous tone in Karen's voice — "we have to go to the other clothes trunk. And it's on *the third floor.*"

If this had been a movie, right at that moment scary music would have sounded. The third floor was, after all, where Karen believed Ben Brewer lived. As it was, the only sound was the nervous tapping of Karen's little foot. She twisted her fingers and bit her lip.

"I don't know," she said.

"We don't *have* to play Let's All Come In," said Jessi.

Well, that decided it for Karen.

"Oh, yes we do," she said with great conviction. "We can't let a *ghost* rule our lives."

Karen took Jessi's hand and squeezed it firmly but bravely.

"Come on," she said.

For her, I think, being scared is half the fun.

Karen led Jessi up the narrow staircase that leads to the third floor of the Brewer mansion. The third floor is seldom used. The house is so big that the first and second floors can comfortably house the whole family, large as it is. The third floor is really only used for storage. It's like one big attic, even though it's sectioned into rooms.

As they neared the top of the stairway, Karen began to creep.

"Aughhh!" she screamed suddenly.

"What is it?" Jessi asked.

Karen's eyes, big as saucers, focused on the top of the bannister. She didn't say anything, she just pointed.

There, in the dust that covered the wood bannister, someone had etched the words "Turn Back!"

"Maybe we should," said Jessi. She didn't believe in the ghost, and yet . . .

"There's no turning back now," Karen said dramatically. She pressed ahead.

Karen crept down the hall to the room where the other trunk was stored. The door was closed, but not completely. It was open a small crack. Karen pushed the door slowly. *CRASH!* A can clattered on the floor in front of them and water splattered from the can all over their shoes and legs.

Of course, Karen screamed again. At this point, though, Jessi began to be skeptical. The door had obviously been booby-trapped. Why would a ghost booby-trap a door with a can full of water? It seemed to Jessi that the tricks a ghost would play would be, somehow, more ghostly. This seemed more like a practical joke. And if she had to name a practical joker in the house, she was pretty sure she knew who that might be.

Karen swung the door open wide and stomped loudly into the room.

"Ben Brewer!" she called out. "We're coming in. You can't stop us. We've made up our minds."

Karen marched over to the large dusty trunk, unlatched it, and opened its lid. The smell of mothballs flooded the room. Karen lifted up a dark blue crushed velvet dress that lay across the top of the pile.

"How about this dre —" she started to say, but her eye caught a note that had been tucked underneath the gown. The note was written in a thick, dark red ink.

"Blood-red," Karen whispered.

She picked up the note and read it.

"Death to all who enter here," it said.

Karen stood frozen, fixed in one spot. Her face paled.

"I think we better go back downstairs," she said to Jessi. Her voice was small and shaking. She dropped the note. It fluttered to the floor. She walked out of the room, gliding, like a sleep-walker or a zombie.

Jessi picked up the note and looked it over. The paper had been torn off a notepad. On the other side was a printed logo.

"SHS," it said.

SHS. Stoneybrook High School.

Jessi folded the note and put it in her pocket. She followed Karen back downstairs.

When Kristy and her mom got home, Karen ran down to the front hallway, frantic to tell them all the latest evidence.

"It *proves*," she said, "that Ben Brewer is living

right up there on the third floor. How do we know he won't come down?" she asked. "How do we know he doesn't want to take over the second floor, too?"

As it happened, Sam and Charlie pulled in the driveway right after Kristy and their mom. When Sam came in, Karen was going on about the ghost.

"The note was written in blood," she said, then shuddered. "I wonder whose."

Sam smirked and nudged Charlie. Mrs. Brewer shot a look at Sam. He shrugged innocently.

"I wonder how another child would fit into all this," Mrs. Brewer wondered aloud.

"Another child?" Kristy asked. "What do you mean?" Mrs. Brewer shrugged distractedly. Kristy shook her head and followed her mom into the kitchen with Karen trailing behind. Jessi pulled the note out of her pocket and handed it to Sam.

"Lose something?" Jessi asked.

Sam grinned sheepishly and shoved the note quickly into his pocket.

Kristy came out of the kitchen.

"Of course this ghost incident will have to be written up in the club notebook," she said. "You realize that all the other club members should be aware of anything this important."

Jessi told me later she just smiled and nodded. Ben Brewer was living in the mansion, all right. It was Sam Thomas who'd made sure of that.

CHAPTER 10

Monday

Dear Stacey,

There you are in New York City and here I am in California. Whatever happened to good ol' Stoneybrook, Connecticut? I'm having the time of my life. It almost seems as if I never left in the first place. The We ♥ Kids Club is keeping me very busy. It's a baby-sitters club with a difference — NO RING DINGS ALLOWED!

Dawn

All that weekend I looked forward to the next meeting of the We ♥ Kids Club. I had had such a good time with Clover and Daffodil, and couldn't wait to tell Sunny and the other members of the club.

When I arrived that Monday afternoon, Sunny was sitting on the floor of her room, with newspapers spread out all around her. She had a bag of potting soil, a couple of small clay pots, and a few jars in which she had rooted some babies from her spider plant.

"Hi. Come in," she said. "If you can find a place. I'm just potting these."

I sprawled out on an empty stretch of Sunny's green shag rug. It was the usual relaxed, California atmosphere of the We ♥ Kids Club.

While we waited for Jill and Maggie, I told Sunny all about my afternoon at the Austins', about Clover's wild imagination, and about Daffodil's tries at the ring toss.

"I think Clover's going to be an actress," said Sunny. "Or a writer or something like that."

"And Daffodil is the real surprise," I said. "You think because she's quiet she's going to be shy, but she has a real determination to her."

"Did you notice how she's suddenly all leg?" Sunny asked. "She's like a colt or a baby deer. . . ."

"Exactly," I laughed.

As we were talking, a warm, homey feeling spread through me. It occurred to me that what we were doing was sharing the exact same kind of information that Kristy has the members of the Baby-sitters Club write up in the official Club notebook. And here we were just talking. Simple as that. See, I thought, you *can* accomplish things informally.

Jill and Maggie arrived together, talking about some kids at school. Sunny finished up her potting.

"Do you remember Joe Luhan?" Jill asked me.

"Sure." He had been one of the boys in my class.

"Well, he and Tom Swanson are having a party on Sunday. Will you still be here or are you leaving before then?"

"The day before," I said. "I'm leaving Saturday."

Too bad. That sounded like fun. A party with Joe Luhan and Tom Swanson. I'd grown up with those guys. I knew them better than I knew most of the boys in Stoneybrook.

Sunny's mom poked her head in the door.

"Am I allowed in here?" she asked.

"*Mo-om,*" Sunny moaned. "Of course. What do you think?"

Her mom looked over at me and smiled.

"It just occurred to me," she said. "Dawn, would you and the girls like to stay for dinner? We won't get many more chances to see you this visit. You're just here for another week, aren't you?"

I looked at Sunny. Sunny looked at me.

"Oh. Stay, stay, stay," Sunny pleaded.

"I'll have to check with Dad," I said. He was back at work that week and wouldn't be home for another half hour. "Can I let you know at the end of the meeting?" I asked Sunny's mom.

"Sure," she said. "If your dad says yes, we'd love to have you." She winked at me. "Spinach lasagna," she said, and she disappeared out the door.

"Yum," said Sunny. "That reminds me. I'm hungry."

"Me too," said Maggie. "Starving."

"Should I get us our snack?" Sunny asked.

"Yeah!" we all agreed.

Sunny stood up and dusted the potting soil off her hands.

"Ick! Wash your hands first," Maggie teased.

Sunny wiggled her muddy fingers in Maggie's face.

"No way!" she laughed, then bounded down the stairs.

Since no phone calls were coming in, we just sat around chatting. Jill and Maggie talked some more about the kids I remembered in our class.

Right then an idea began taking seed in my mind. I started to picture myself back in the class, and how easy it would be to slip right back in.

Sunny came back up with the food — guacamole dip and cut-up raw vegetables that she had made earlier in the afternoon.

"All *right*," Jill said, grabbing a carrot stick.

"No calls yet?" Sunny asked.

We shook our heads. The phone hadn't rung once.

"Maybe we should work on the recipe file," Sunny suggested.

This was a project I hadn't heard about yet. Sunny pulled a yellow plastic file box off the top of her desk. On the front she had pasted a picture of a bright red apple. Inside were cards with recipes that kids could make and that they liked to eat.

"Healthy recipes," said Sunny. "It's an extension of that cookbook I showed you."

"Wow!" I said. "What a great idea."

Maggie and Jill fished into their purses and each pulled out a recipe she had found over the weekend. Jill's homemade lemonade was from a magazine. Maggie's "Raisin Surprise" was from the back of a raisin box. They set about copying the recipes onto the small yellow index cards.

Sunny chomped on a celery stick and looked at me. "It'd be great if you can stay for dinner," she said.

I thought back to all the times in the past that I had had dinner over at Sunny's house. How many times had it been? Probably a thousand. Well, at least a hundred. Sunny's mom and dad were great. When we were younger they always let us be excused from the table as soon as we had finished eating, just so we would have a longer time to play.

"I hope you can stay," Sunny said again, and suddenly something popped into my head.

Maybe I *could* stay. Maybe I could *really* stay. Maybe I didn't have to go back to Connecticut at all, or just go back to get my things. Maybe I could move back in with Dad and Jeff, have my old room back, my old friends, my old school.

It was a strange thought, scary and exciting at the same time. Until then, I had just been having a great time, a *fabulous* time, but it had never occurred to me that I could think about making it last forever (or at least for longer). Now that the thought occurred to me, what was I supposed to do?

I was still sitting in the same room, but it felt like I was in another world. Around me, I could hear Sunny and Jill and Maggie chattering away.

Jill rummaged around in her purse for her bottle of nail polish, a different color this time. The phone rang, a call came in. I think it was one of the neighbors down the street, and Maggie took the job.

"Earth to Dawn. Earth to Dawn," said Sunny. She had her hands cupped over her mouth like a megaphone.

"Oh, yeah," I said. "I'm here." (Just barely.)

"So what do you think?"

"About what?"

"About the *nail* polish."

"What about it?"

"Do you think Berry Pink is better on Jill or Lucious Blush?"

Hmm, I guess I had missed a part of the conversation. I took a look. Jill had half of the old polish on and half of the new.

"Which is which?" I asked.

"Forget it," Jill giggled. "They'll *discontinue* the colors before you decide."

"What time is it?" I asked suddenly.

"Five-thirty," said Sunny. "Hey, you can call your dad now."

Five-thirty. Time to leave.

"I don't think I can stay for dinner," I said abruptly. "I have to do something. I mean, I have to talk to Dad about something."

"But . . ." Sunny started.

The phone rang again.

"It's Mrs. Austin," she said. "She needs someone for Clover and Daffodil. Do you want it?" she asked me.

"Yeah," I said. "Of course. Thanks. Sign me up. But I gotta run."

Sunny and the others stared after me. I grabbed my purse and ran out the door. It must've all looked very strange. Well, what can I say? It felt strange for me, too. Suddenly it seemed like my whole world was changing.

CHAPTER 11

                                    Monday
   Dear Mom,
       I'm ~~writing to~~ talk about
       I ~~just want to say~~ that
       this is a ~~very~~ difficult
       ~~thing for me~~ to

W ell, that was a card I never finished writing.
How do you tell your mother that you want to
move away from her? That you want, in fact,
to move to the other side of the country?

   When I came back from the We ♥ Kids meeting I ran right to my room. I thought it might help
if I wrote a draft of a letter to Mom and figured
out how I might approach this very delicate subject. As you see, I didn't get very far.

I decided, really, that it was too early to think about Mom. The first step was just to talk to Dad.

Jeff knocked on my door to call me to dinner.

"Hey, Sis," he said. "Get your bod to the table."

How could I get through life without my dopey brother, I wondered. I didn't *want* to leave Jeff. I didn't *want* to leave Dad.

Mrs. Bruen had made her usual terrific dinner (fish fillets baked with tomatoes and covered with cheese sauce), and we ate it in the beautiful, clean dining room at a table with a tablecloth and flowers. Everything was arranged nicely, everything was organized. No misplaced purses, no lost keys.

I poured myself some juice from the frosty cold pitcher.

"Broccoli?" Dad asked me.

"Yes, please."

How would I start?

"Dad," I began.

"Yes?"

"I was thinking. . . ."

"Yes?"

"Um . . . Um . . . Hmm. I forgot what I was going to say."

Call me chicken if you want. It was very difficult for me to bring up the subject. We ate awhile, and I let Jeff and Dad talk.

"Aw, come on," Jeff was saying. "All my friends get to watch more television than *that*."

"Not on school nights," Dad said firmly. "Enjoy this vacation schedule while you can."

"But, Dad . . ."

"You heard me," said Dad. "Subject closed."

That quieted Jeff. It also gave me space to try again.

"Dad," I said.

"Yeah?"

"I was thinking. . . ."

"Sounds familiar," Dad grinned.

"Yeah, well, I was thinking . . . I mean, it's just an idea, but I was wondering if . . . well, what I'm thinking is, maybe I want to consider, well, maybe I want to consider staying in California, moving here like Jeff did."

I paused. Nobody said anything.

"It's just that I like it so much here," I continued. "Everything is just my style. The weather, the kids. I mean, I just got this idea today, but actually maybe it's been brewing all along. I'm not even sure it's what I want. But I'm thinking about it, so I wanted to bring it up."

Dad was watching me closely. Jeff was watching Dad.

Dad let out a big breath. You'd have thought he was the one doing all the talking.

"Well," he said slowly. "It's certainly a possibility."

Jeff tossed his napkin in the air. He'd been waiting for Dad's response.

"Yippee!" he cried.

"Well," Dad sighed again. "There's a lot to think about here."

It suddenly occurred to me that maybe Dad didn't want me. He didn't seem too enthusiastic. But then he burst into a grin, the kind of grin that's unmistakably his.

"Oh, Sunshine," he said. "You know how happy I would be if you were out here?"

"Yippee!" Jeff yelled again.

"Of course," Dad added quickly, "there's a lot of things we have to consider here. There's your mother. . . ." There was a long pause. "And the custody and your school. And, of course, what *you* really want."

"But it's possible?" I asked.

"Well, from a practical standpoint, yes," Dad said. "You've got your own room here. Mrs. Bruen is already here and working. . . . But from a legal standpoint, I don't know. Your mother has custody, but then, she still has custody of Jeff and here he is. I'd have to talk to her and see, uh, see what we could arrange. Do you want me to call her tonight, just to talk?"

"No!" I was surprised at the strength of my answer.

"Do *you* want to call her?" Dad asked.

"Not yet," I said. I wasn't ready for that at all. "The first thing is I have to figure things out, decide what I want."

"You're the only one who *can* decide that, Sunshine," said Dad. "Your mother and I have the legal proceedings to work out, but we've got to know that it's what you want."

"Right," I said.

Dad and I ate the rest of our dinner in relative silence. You wouldn't have noticed the quiet, though. Jeff did a good job of filling that in.

"If you stay here we can go to the beach all the time," he said enthusiastically. "You can come to my school if I'm in an assembly. I can borrow your Walkman, you can borrow my camera. . . ."

Jeff went on like that for the rest of the meal, but I hardly heard him. All the things I had to think about were swimming through my head.

When I finished dinner I went back to my room and closed the door. California, Connecticut. California, Connecticut. I couldn't keep my thoughts straight. I decided to write them down.

I tore a piece of paper off my notepad and drew a line down the middle. At the top of the left half I wrote PROS: CALIFORNIA. At the top of the right I wrote PROS: STONEYBROOK. When I finished my list, this is what I had:

PROS: CALIFORNIA	PROS: STONEYBROOK
Dad	Mom
Jeff	
the sun!	
We ♥ Kids Club	Baby-sitters Club
Sunny (and others)	Mary Anne (and others)
healthy foods	
the beach	
an organized household	
Clover and Daffodil	the kids in Stoneybrook

I thought about adding "Disneyland" under "California" but decided against it. It didn't seem like enough of a reason to move from one coast to the other, and besides, the California side already had plenty of entries.

Well then, it seemed pretty clear. California. I guess that's what I wanted. Somehow, though, it didn't seem resolved in my head. I needed to talk about it some more. I couldn't talk about it with Mom, and I'd already talked about it some with Dad. Maybe I should call Sunny? I decided against it. She'd just persuade me to stay. Maybe Mary Anne . . . Of course. She'd *said* to call.

I wandered out of my room.

"Dad," I called. "Can I call Mary Anne in Connecticut?"

"It's ten o'clock there," he said.

It was late, but it was vacation, so she should still be awake.

"Can I?" I asked again.

"Sure," he said.

The kitchen was now empty, so I set myself up in there. I opened my address book to the "S" page and ran my finger across. Mary Anne's name was the first. She had, after all, been my first Stoneybrook friend.

As I dialed her number, I could almost hear her voice answering the phone. She'd probably squeal when she heard it was me. Mary Anne was a good choice, I thought. She'd be perfect to talk to in a situation like this. She's the kind of friend who would help me figure out what *I* wanted. I mean, of course she'd be sad if I wanted to stay in California, but she'd understand.

On the other end, the phone was ringing. Three rings. Four. No one picked up. Maybe they're just pulling into the driveway, I thought. I let it ring more. No one answered. I laid the phone back in its cradle and dropped down in a kitchen chair.

Around me the light was getting softer. The kitchen took on a rosy hue. Ten o'clock in Connecticut. I pictured Mary Anne and her father coming home from wherever they were, turning the lights on in their darkened house. Then I pictured Mom. I wondered what she was doing. Probably she was reading in bed. Or maybe she was out with the Trip-Man. (Horrors!) I wondered what she would say when I told her what I was thinking about. What would she do in that funny old farmhouse all by herself? If only *she* could move back to California, too.

Of course, I knew that was impossible.

The hard thing was, I found myself realizing that the person I really wanted to be talking to about all this *was* Mom. I wanted the two of us to be sitting on my bed, having one of our heart-to-hearts. I wanted her to ask me questions, say wise things. I wanted her to help lead me through all this tangle I seemed to be tied up in.

I started to feel closed in from all the things I had to think about. I went out to the back patio and watched the golden sun fade.

CHAPTER 12

Dear Dawn,
 It's business as usual at the Pikes'.
The other morning I sat there with
Mallory, and wouldn't you know it,
the triplets were on Nicky's back.
Nicky ran off to you-know-where
and eventually I had to go get him.
Sound familiar?

Love
Kristy

P.S. Nicky talked a lot about you,
 actually. I think he really misses
 you. Well, he doesn't have long to
 wait now.

I got the postcard from Kristy that Tuesday, when I still hadn't made up my mind what to do. I didn't find out the details until later, but I could picture the scene at the Pike household, where things are always a little wild.

The Pikes, you may remember, have eight kids. And that's just one family, not two combined or anything like that. Because it's such a crowd, Mrs. Pike always gets two sitters whenever she goes out. Now that Mallory, the oldest Pike, is eleven and in the Baby-sitters Club, Mrs. Pike usually uses Mallory plus one other sitter. That day it was Kristy.

Claire, the youngest Pike (she's all of five years old), let Kristy in. She was still in her pajamas.

"Moozie!" she cried. ("Moozie" is what she sometimes calls her mom.) "Moozie! Kristy's here."

Moozie didn't appear, but Mallory did.

"Mom'll be down in a minute," she said.

"Where's everybody else?" asked Kristy. (The house seemed strangely quiet.)

"The triplets and Nicky are in the backyard, and Vanessa and Margo are upstairs."

"Well," said Kristy. "Where should we start? How about with you, Claire? Let's get you out of those pajamas and into your play clothes."

"These *are* my play clothes, Kristy silly-billy-goo-goo," said Claire. "Today I'm wearing my pajamas *all day long.*"

Kristy looked at Mallory. Mallory shrugged. That's another thing about the Pikes. Mr. and Mrs. Pike hardly have any rules. If Claire were going to school that day, of course she'd have to get dressed. But for staying at home? If pajamas was what she wanted, pajamas it was.

Claire streaked up the stairs, waggling her head and crying "Moo!" Was she calling her mother or making cow sounds? Did it matter? This was definitely going to be one of Claire's sillier days.

The back door swung open and the triplets appeared. They each grabbed a cookie from the jar on the kitchen counter and then raced back outside. The door swung open again. It was Nicky. He'd come for *his* cookie. (The triplets are ten and Nicky is eight. He sometimes has a hard time keeping up.) *BANG!* Nicky was back out the door, following his brothers.

"Kristy, hi!" It was Mrs. Pike. In her hurry, she grabbed a sweater out of the closet. "Oops, that's Vanessa's," she said. She grabbed another. "I should be back early afternoon. More library business. And if the meeting gets out on time, I'm going to squeeze in a haircut."

She gave the sitters last-minute instructions and reminded Mallory that there was canned ravioli and homemade cole slaw for lunch.

Ravioli and *cole slaw?* Well, I guess, when you're getting meals together for eight kids every day, you come up with some pretty unusual combinations.

Mrs. Pike called good-bye over her shoulder and hurried out the door.

"I'll go let Vanessa and Margo know I'm here," Kristy said to Mallory.

To keep all fronts covered, Mallory headed out to the yard.

Vanessa and Margo are two of the middle kids. Vanessa is nine and Margo is seven. You can pretty much trust them to play well by themselves, but you always have to check to see what they're up to. In this case that was a good idea. Claire had joined them and Vanessa was showing her sisters how to write a letter in "invisible ink." She had dragged a carton of milk upstairs and the three of them were dipping paintbrushes into the milk and using it as ink to write messages on white paper.

"Kristy!" Vanessa said when she walked in. "Read my message. Can you, please? It's invisible, like the seas." (Vanessa is a budding poet. She loves to rhyme and doesn't always care so much about making sense.)

Kristy looked at the blank sheet of paper.

"A polar bear in a snowstorm?" she guessed.

"Silly-billy-goo-goo!" cried Claire.

"No, it's a message," said Vanessa. She held the paper flat and blew on it so the milk would dry. "You can't see it now," she said, "but watch this."

She strode out of the bedroom and into her parents' room, where there was an iron and an ironing board standing up in the corner.

"Heat," she said. "We'll iron the messages and the heat will make the milk letters turn brown."

"Wait a minute. Wait a minute," said Kristy. "I'll be the one to do the ironing."

"But I iron all the time," said Vanessa. "For Mom. I do practically a basket a week."

Kristy considered.

"Well," she said. "You can iron, but I'll supervise. Claire and Margo, you sit over here and watch."

Kristy sat on the edge of the bed and patted places next to her for the two younger girls.

Vanessa waited for the iron to heat up and then ran it lightly over the sheets of paper. As she predicted, the white letters darkened and the messages came clear.

Vanessa's message read:

"Ships on the ocean,
Ships at shore,
Wipe your feet,
And close the door."

Margo's said, "My teacher is a big baboon."

Claire's just said, "CAT HAT RAT FAT CLAIRE." (Well, when you're first learning to write, you don't have a lot of words to choose from.)

"Let's write some for the boys!" Vanessa cried suddenly. She started out the door.

"Hey! Iron off," Kristy reminded her. (When you're a baby-sitter you *do* have to be thinking about safety all the time.)

Vanessa ran back and unplugged the iron, and the girls ran back to their room to write more secret messages.

By the time lunch rolled around, the girls had a stack of paper a few inches high. Each of the pieces had a secret milk-message written on it. It had been a busy morning.

Mallory was in the kitchen heating up the ravioli. (She had opened a giant-sized can. It looked like it was meant for an army platoon.) Kristy started dishing up the cole slaw.

"Nicky's in a little bit of a funk," Mallory said, filling Kristy in on the backyard crew. "The triplets wouldn't let him play with them."

"Again?" said Kristy. This was an ongoing problem.

"Well, they were playing Frisbee and all they'd let him do was fetch it when it went out of the yard."

Nicky banged through the door and into the kitchen. He slumped into a chair and began to kick his feet back and forth.

"Hi, Nicky," said Kristy.

"Hi," Nicky said glumly.

The triplets trooped in behind him.

"Ravioli?" said Byron. "Cole slaw? Ugh!" But he sat right down at the table, and Kristy noticed that when she put his plate in front of him, he gobbled the food right up.

"We've got secret messages for you," Margo said to the boys. She handed Jordan the stack of papers.

"Who cares?" he said. He pushed the papers aside.

"Look at them," Vanessa said. "They've got secret messages on them. Bet you can't read them."

"Don't want to," said Jordan.

Margo grabbed the papers up.

"Well, don't then," she said. "We don't care."

Adam had taken his spoon to his plate and was mixing the ravioli in with the cole slaw.

"Ooh, gross," he said. "Snake guts."

Nicky grinned.

"Hey, that's what it does look like," he said. "The tomato sauce is the blood."

Unfortunately, when Nicky said that, he had a full mouth of ravioli himself, and some of it splurted out on the table.

"Yuk!" Adam cried. "Ooh, Nicky! Say it, don't spray it!"

Nicky sat there quietly for a moment. Kristy thought he might be about to burst into tears. Instead, he looked at her and said, "May I please be excused? I want to go to the hideout."

Now, there's an example of one of the few rules in the Pike house. Nicky is allowed to go to the hideout only if he tells whoever is in charge where he's going.

"Eat some more ravioli first," said Mallory.

Nicky did, and he was excused.

The hideout that he disappeared to was the secret passage I told you about, the one that's in my house. Nicky goes in through the trapdoor in our barn. He usually just sits in there, reads or whatever. It's his special place.

That day, a half hour passed, then forty-five minutes. Lunch was cleared and cleaned up and the kids all went outside together to play in the backyard. Kristy decided she'd go check on Nicky. He was right where he said he would be, sitting alone at the head of the tunnel. Kristy climbed down the ladder and joined him.

"Hey, Nick," she said.

"Hi."

"Whatcha doin'?"

"Nothin'."

It took Kristy awhile to get Nicky talking, but they did talk some about how hard it sometimes was to be a younger brother.

"This feels like when Dawn talked to me," Nicky said.

I was the one who first discovered Nicky's hiding place. And when I found him, we had had a pretty good heart-to-heart.

"You miss Dawn?" Kristy asked.

Nicky nodded. "Will she be back soon?"

"At the end of the week," Kristy said.

Nicky heaved a big sigh.

"I don't know if I can last," he said.

Kristy laughed and gave him a hug.

"Come on," she said. "We better get going."

Back at the Pikes' house, things were as hectic as before. The only difference was, Mrs. Pike had come home.

"There's my Nicholas," she smiled.

She gave her son a quick kiss on the cheek and kneaded his slumping shoulders.

"You didn't get a haircut," Kristy noticed.

"No time," said Mrs. Pike. "Guess I'll have to call you again."

She paid Kristy and Mallory and left to check the backyard.

Hearing about the Pikes and reading Kristy's postcard got me thinking about the Baby-sitters Club and all the other big jobs we take on. "No job too big, no job too crazy" — that should be our motto. A lot of times it even seems the more chaotic, the more fun. In a way, I'm kind of proud of that. Whenever a problem has cropped up, we've pulled a solution from somewhere, out of our hats if we had to.

Listen to me. I sound like a testimonial.

Of course, the P.S. on Kristy's card helped. So Nicky Pike missed me, huh? Well, what do you know. . . . The truth was, I sort of missed him, too.

CHAPTER 13

Dear Dawn,

Miss you so much, honey. The old house just isn't the same without you. You'll be pleased (?) to know that I've had date after date with Trip. We've gone to a chamber concert, and a wine tasting, and I'll see him again Friday night before you get home. This time we're off to a lecture on humor.

Dawn, the very thought of picking you up at the airport has me all in smiles. A big hug and kiss for my sweet firstborn girl.

Love,
Mom

A lecture on humor? Oh, give me a break. How could Mom be falling for Trip-Man? That was *exactly* the problem with him. He'd be just the type to go to a *lecture* about humor. That's because he has no sense of it himself. Compare him with Dad. Dad is fun and funny. The Trip-Man is a bore.

I got the postcard from Mom on Wednesday, and no, I still hadn't made up my mind what to do. That wasn't the only postcard that came for me in the mail. There was also one from Jessi.

Dear Dawn,

Last night my family and I went back to visit our old neighborhood. It was fun, but also strange. All the relatives and all the old friends ... It was great to see them, but in a way, it made me think — where is home? I guess it's Stoneybrook now. This is pretty heavy — I hope you don't mind my writing you. It's just that I figured you're sort of going through the same thing, too.

See you soon,
Jessi

Well, what a haul in the mail. You can see why it was hard for me to make up my mind. My mom's postcard got me all agitated, but that got me thinking. I certainly did feel involved in the whole Trip-Man thing. I wanted to run right back to Connecticut so I could keep my eye on the situation. Did I want the Trip-Man marrying my mother? Moving into *our* farmhouse? No way!

Then, of course, Jessi's postcard . . . I never thought of it before, but she and I really *were* in very similar situations. Of course, Jessi went back to a neighborhood where everyone is Black, and I went back to one where everyone is . . . well, blond. I thought of all my friends in the Baby-sitters Club. We all *were* very different — our backgrounds, the way we look, our interests. There was something very nice about that. Maybe Mary Anne doesn't read all the ghost stories that I happen to like, but what did that matter? And Claudia — she does eat a lot of junk food, all right, but she draws beautifully. I remembered the slumber party they had given me before I left. I pictured Claudia sitting on her sleeping bag, sketching Jessi, whose legs were stretched long, like a real ballerina's. This sounds corny, but the scene was like an advertisement for the U.N. or something. Different kinds of people with different interests, all getting along beautifully. (Okay, getting along *most* of the time.)

I headed over to Sunny's to spend the afternoon. I decided to talk with her about my dilemma.

"Dawn!" she squealed when I told her. "You're going to stay in California!"

"I didn't say that," I said defensively. "I said I was *thinking* about it."

"What's there to think about?" said Sunny. She picked up the California/Connecticut list that I had brought along with me. "It's all right here on paper. The vote is in."

"It's not that simple," I said. "Different things on the list have different weights."

"Okay," she said, looking down the list. "Your dad and Jeff. They balance your mom."

Well, sort of. How could I ever rate something like that?

"And the We ♥ Kids Club balances the Baby-sitters Club," Sunny went on.

"Maybe not," I said carefully.

"Dawn, you told me yourself that you love how relaxed the club is here."

"Yeah."

That's what I said, but what I thought was the We ♥ Kids Club is not really as busy or as involved or active somehow as the Baby-sitters Club. Of course, I couldn't say that to Sunny's face. Instead, I just sort of shrugged my shoulders.

"Okay, another item," said Sunny. "Sunny (and others) versus Mary Anne (and others). I guess that balances, right?"

"Right," I said, halfheartedly. Was Sunny really as good a friend now as Mary Anne was? And really, I had five other friends in the Baby-sitters Club. Six, counting Stacey. I was much closer with all of them than I was with Jill and Maggie. Same with the kids I baby-sat for. Did Clover and Daffodil balance out all the kids in Stoneybrook? The Pikes, Jamie and Lucy Newton, the Perkins girls, Kristy's brothers and sister . . .

"Okay," said Sunny. "Here we go. The sun. The beach. Healthy foods. An organized household."

One by one she ticked off all the pros for California.

"Dawn, it's obvious. You're a California girl," she said.

"I know."

"And a California girl *belongs* in California."

I felt my face tighten. All of a sudden I didn't feel like discussing the subject anymore.

"You know what?" I said. "Let's drop this. I think it's better if I think about this whole thing myself."

"Okay," said Sunny. She looked a little taken aback.

That evening, when I went home for dinner, Dad was waiting to talk to me.

"Well, Sunshine," he said. "Is the verdict in?"

"Oh, Dad, not yet," I moaned.

Dad wrinkled up his forehead in concern.

"I know it's a big decision," he said, "but you're scheduled to fly back on Saturday. If you're really thinking about staying, I'll have to talk with your mother, well, the latest by tomorrow. We'll have to cancel the plane reservation, make other arrangements."

"Can I let you know tomorrow?" I asked. "Just one more day?"

Dad paused a long time.

"Oh, Sunshine," he said. "I don't want to influence your decision. You know what I would love, but there're many considerations here. Take the night to decide, but I really do have to know by tomorrow."

"Oh, thanks, Daddy," I said. I gave him the biggest hug ever.

Dad threw his arm around me and we walked into the kitchen to sit down for yet another terrific meal. The sun was streaming in through the skylight and the terra cotta tiles were cool and sparkling under our feet. (Mrs. Bruen had just given them one of her good moppings.)

After dinner Jeff and I helped with the dishes and then Dad brought a deck of cards out back. The three of us sat down at the picnic table for a game of Crazy Eights.

From where I sat I could see Clover and Daffodil next door, running around their yard barefoot, playing tag. I could smell the smokey scent of grilled fish coming from the barbecue of our other neighbors. A soft breeze rustled the skirt of my sundress against my warm, bare legs.

It'd be nice if Mom were here, I found myself thinking. If she were a part of things, playing cards with me, puttering around the patio. And wouldn't it be great if the doorbell rang and it was Mary Anne, just dropping by for a visit. What I wanted was to be able to share all the *things* I loved with all the *people* I loved. I imagined Nicky Pike out here holing up in a new, California hiding place. Maybe in the crawl space between the bushes. Maybe in the cave down by the creek.

That night, as I lay in bed, I made my decision. I knew what I had to do, where I had to be. I fell asleep hugging my pillow. I slept the whole night soundly, undisturbed.

CHAPTER 14

Dear Dawn,

Kristy says you will be back on Saturday. If you hear a noise in the secret passage, don't get scared. It'll just be me. Lately I have a lot of ghost-hunting to do there. It keeps me busy.

Your secret tunnel pal,

Nicky

P.S You think maybe Sunday we could search the tunnel for old coins?

Thursday I woke up after Dad had already gone to work. I spent the day riding bikes with Jeff and came home to Nicky's funny note. Of course, I knew what I was going to do and by that point I was bursting to tell.

When Dad came home from work I sat him down to prepare him for my decision.

"I've decided to leave California and go back to Connecticut," I said.

Phew! Was that ever a hard thing to get out.

"I like both places," I continued. "I like them a lot. But I've made my home at Mom's now. It's time for me to go back."

Dad's eyes were all misty as I was explaining.

"I know," he said. "I guess I knew it all along."

Jeff, who had been standing in the doorway, turned around and stomped down the hall. It would take him another day or two to adjust to the disappointment.

"Well," said Dad, "for such a young girl you've had a big decision to make. You've got two homes. Just remember — this is always your home, too. We'll always be in touch, you can always visit. Your room here is reserved. And so is your place in our hearts."

Oh, Dad! What a cornball. By the time he finished his speech, my eyes were all misty, too. Okay, they were more than misty. Tears were streaming down my cheeks like rain.

"Dad," I blubbered. "Can I call Mom?"

"Sure, Sunshine," he said.

He left the room so I could be alone.

I think Mom was surprised to hear my voice all shaken up.

"I was wondering," I asked her. "Could you bring Mary Anne along to the airport with you?"

"Of course," said Mom. "I'll call her up as soon as we hang up."

Mom stopped talking. So did I.

"Dawn, honey," she said. "Is everything all right?"

Well, I hadn't meant to tell Mom that I had been thinking about staying in California, but somehow it all came flooding out.

"You know how it is, Mom," I said. "Avocados, the beach . . ."

"Oh, Dawn," she said, "I knew when you went out there you'd start thinking about moving back."

How come everybody seemed to know more about me than *I* knew? Dad had known I was going to decide to go back to Stoneybrook. Mom knew I was going to think about staying in California in the first place. Parents!

"You know, Dawn," Mom continued, "if you *do* want to stay in California, we could give it some thought. I know it's been difficult for you. I know you love it out there."

"I made my decision," I said. My voice was cracking. "I'm going to come home."

"Dawn," Mom blubbered. "I would've missed you so much."

We certainly were a weepy family that night. Yup, the four of us were a family, even though we were split up in two different houses and separated by thousands of miles. And as far as understanding goes, I sure got a lot of that from my parents. From both of them. My dad might be on one coast and my mom on the other but, parent-wise, I guess I'm pretty lucky.

Friday, my last full day in California, was a pretty busy day. That morning I baby-sat one last time for Clover and Daffodil. Daffodil asked if she could write me. And Clover (always Clover) told me she might come visit me by spaceship. When Mrs. Austin came home, she slipped a thin package into my hand along with my pay.

"What is it?" I asked.

"Open it and see," she smiled.

Inside was a hand-woven purse that Mrs. Austin had made and lined in silk. The threads were red and a deep golden color.

"Like sunshine," she said. I blushed. Had Dad told her my nickname?

After the job, I ran over to Sunny's house for one last meeting of the We ♥ Kids Club. Actually, it was more like a party, a good-bye party for me. Sunny, Jill, and Maggie had made all kinds of treats — fresh pineapple wedges, zucchini bread, carrot cake. They had a big tray of food that they set down in the center of our circle.

Sunny banged her hand on the floor, like a gavel.

"This party will now come to order," she teased.

Believe me, there was no need to call us to the food.

The party was interrupted only twice by job calls. Maggie took one and Jill took the other.

There really wasn't enough work here to go around, I thought. In a way, it was good I was leaving.

When the "meeting" adjourned, Sunny pulled two packages out from under her bed.

"Surprise!" she said. "You can't go without your presents."

I *knew* it. I knew Sunny couldn't say good-bye to me without *some* sort of surprise.

One package, the first, was a book, I could feel it. I tore open the wrapping paper. *Kids Can Cook . . . Naturally.*

"Thanks, you guys," I said enthusiastically. "This is great!"

"Open the other," said Sunny.

The other was my very own recipe file. The three of them had made it for me. The file box itself was blue, and they had pasted a picture of a sun on front. Inside were all their recipes, copied in their three different handwritings.

"You guys!" I cried. "You guys!"

What I was trying to say was, I just loved it.

I said good-bye to everybody. Then it was time for me to head home, for my last dinner with the California branch of the Schafer family.

Dad and I had discussed it, and we'd decided that, for the last night, it would be fun to go out. Dad had suggested a Mexican restaurant, a big favorite of mine and usually a favorite of Jeff's, too. Jeff, though, was still a little upset. He was my last hurdle, the last peace I had left to make. As we drove to the restaurant, Jeff kept a pouty look on his face. He squinted his eyes and puckered his mouth.

"What're you going to order, Jeff?" Dad asked in an effort to draw him out.

"Dunno," said Jeff.

"How about chicken enchiladas? You always like those."

"Yuk," said Jeff.

Dad and I exchanged quick smiles.

When we got to the restaurant, Jeff began twisting his fingers into the hem of the tablecloth.

"Dawn," he said sullenly. "How come you're leaving? Is it because we're boys?"

"No," I laughed. Jeff looked hurt. I tried to look as solemn as I could. "You thought I was leaving because you and Dad are boys? Not at all. I just have to go back."

"Maybe you can visit Dawn this summer," Dad suggested.

"Maybe she could come back and visit again *here*," Jeff insisted.

Jeff would always be true to California.

"Anyway, I had a good time with you," he said grudgingly.

"So did I." I smiled back.

"I liked when I took your picture at Disneyland," he said. "And I liked when I dropped the crab in your lap at the beach."

The very thought perked Jeff right up. Despite himself, he started to smile.

"Hey, how come you and your friends all wear those bikinis, anyway?" he asked. "Those things are really gross."

I had to laugh. And so did Dad.

When the waiter came, Jeff didn't even bother to look at the menu.

"Chicken enchiladas," he said.

That's our Jeff.

The meals came and we all ate hungrily. Dad ordered coffee before we left.

"You really can come back any time you want, Sunshine," he said. "Anytime during the summer, any vacation."

He took a sip from his cup.

"And hey," he said, suddenly inspired. "Why not bring all those friends of yours? All your friends in the Baby-sitters Club. I've certainly heard enough about them."

"Really?" I asked.

"How many would that be?" he calculated. "Six?"

"Six girls!" Jeff choked. "No way!"

"And all of them baby-sitters," Dad laughed. "Jeff, they'd have you corralled in no time."

The Baby-sitters Club in California? It was a *great* idea.

"Could I really bring them?" I asked. "When?"

"When?" Dad smiled. "Whenever!"

CHAPTER 15

Saturday

Dear Dad and Jeff,

Hello from me (and from John Wayne, too!) I'm curled up in my window seat, watching the west disappear beneath me. Well, as you said, Dad, it's only a plane ride away. But how come it's such a long plane ride?

Jeff, I hope you write me. Keep me posted about school, Clover and Daffodil, and, of course, the most important thing — what Mrs. Bruen makes for dinner! (Just so I can eat my heart out.)

I love you both. I'll miss you a lot. Thanks for a fabu-ful, wonder-ific time.

Dawn

Well, it was C-Day again, only this time "C" stood for Connecticut, not California. That morning we had to get up pretty early to get me to my flight — because of the time change, the plane east leaves much earlier than the one going west. The neighborhood was quiet when we woke up, and the three of us sat groggily at the breakfast table, slowly coming awake.

"Mmm, coffee," Dad said, sipping from his cup.

That's about all the conversation any of us could muster.

When we got to the airport and got me all checked in, Jeff didn't want us to go to the gate.

"Wait! Let me take your picture by the John Wayne statue," he said. "Wait! Don't you want to buy another postcard?"

I think he thought that if he stalled long enough, I would miss my flight and then I would just stay in California forever.

Dad rested his hands on Jeff's shoulders.

"We'd better get your sister to her plane," he said. "Flights don't wait for passengers buying postcards."

By the time we got through the metal detector and to the gate, the flight was already boarding. Dad gave me a last big hug.

"You take care now, Sunshine," he said. "And don't go forgetting about your California family."

"Don't worry, Dad," I laughed.

Jeff was shifting from one foot to the other.

"Come on," he said. "The plane's gonna leave."

I think now that he knew I was really going to go, he just wanted to get the whole thing over with. But as I got in line and was waiting for the flight attendant to take my ticket, Jeff called after me.

"Hey, Dawn!" he said.

I turned around.

"Smile!" he called. Jeff took my picture one last time, then gave an awkward little wave.

I went through the door and boarded the plane.

Out of one world and back to another. I was a little choked up as I found my way to my seat. I had a window again, this time over the wing. Outside, on the runway, the heat was already shimmering off the asphalt. I wondered what the weather was like in Connecticut.

I dug my hands deep into the pockets of my cotton jacket, just for comfort, I think. Inside one I felt a little slip of paper. I pulled it out.

"Cat Dancing,
Romeo in Joliet,
Scheherazade's Tales," it read.

Hmm. What was tha —? Oh, yes, the list of plays that Tom, my seatmate, had written down for me exactly two weeks before.

I found myself wondering whether Tom might be on my same flight back also. It wasn't impossible. Maybe his auditions had taken two full weeks. I glanced around at the other passengers on the plane, looking for Tom's sandy hair and fair complexion. The flight was not very crowded. There were lots of empty seats. I didn't spot Tom, but as I glanced back toward the kitchen in the rear, I spotted . . . Oh, no! That stewardess! I crunched down in my seat and covered my eyes. I bet she was assigned to my area. It was fate! There was no escape!

Sure enough, when it was time for the safety demonstration, there was the Kewpie doll, right at the head of my row.

Well, there was only one thing to do. I waited until we had taxied to the runway, had taken off, and were safely in the air. When the "Fasten seat belt" sign clicked off, I gathered up my carry-on bag and the blanket I had tucked around my legs. I glanced behind me. The flight attendants were back in the rear, preparing beverage carts, or whatever they do back there. I made my way up the aisle and across, to the other side of the plane.

Since there were lots of empty seats I plunked myself down at another window. I stowed my bag, tucked the blanket up around me, and started the postcard to Dad and Jeff. (I had saved one last John Wayne postcard and decided to use that. I knew it would make Jeff smile.)

When the beverage cart came around, I had a regular, nice stewardess, one who even gave me extra orange juice when I asked for it. I threw a glance back at my old row. My old friend was at work, all right. I could see a passenger trying to wave her down. She had passed that person just as, two weeks ago, she had passed me.

Me, I was safe on the other side of the plane. Two weeks older and two weeks wiser. I smiled and went back to my postcard.

As the plane droned on, I got kind of sleepy. I don't think I'd ever really woken up that morning. My eyes started to slip shut and I think I slept through a lot of the flight.

I did wake up for the movie, though. It was (can you believe it?) *Adventures in Baby-sitting*. Hurray! That got me thinking about all my friends waiting for me at home. I couldn't *wait* to see Mary Anne and, of course, Claudia, Kristy, Jessi, and Mallory, too. And then there were all the kids I sat for. I wondered if Nicky Pike really would come over on Sunday to explore the tunnel with me. I wondered if Mary Anne might want to come, too.

Going home felt very exciting all of a sudden. It really was home I was going to, too. "One home out of two," as Dad had put it, but I sure did have a lot of ties there.

I started thinking about Mom and how glad I would be to see her. I had packed her some avocados in my luggage, the wrinkly, dark green California kind. I'd picked out ones that weren't yet ripe, so she could eat them all next week. A little piece of California for Mom, because I knew she missed it sometimes, too.

I looked at my watch and set it ahead to East Coast time. Right about then Mom would probably be darting around the house, looking for this and that. I hoped she would remember to pick up Mary Anne and bring her along, like she said she would. With Mom, you just never knew.

When we had watched the movie and eaten our meals, the pilot came over the loudspeaker and told us about the weather on the East Coast.

"A light rain is falling," he said. "But the sun is apparently trying to peek through."

Exactly, I thought with a smile. That's Connecticut. (The sun, of course, was me.)

As we started our descent, my stomach got

butterflies. It always does for arrival. I don't know if it's the descent of the plane, or the anticipation of arriving somewhere, but I always feel it.

When we finally landed, I jumped into the aisle, ready to race out the door. The people in front of me were blocking my way. One was reaching into the overhead luggage compartment and handing each bag — slowly — down to the other. "Come on!" I thought impatiently. I was ready to *burst* off that plane!

"Dawn!" a voice called out to me as I came through the door. It was Mom. She broke through the crowd, ran to me, and threw her arms around me. I was so glad just to see her — that Mom face of hers, that funny smile, and that pretty, light, curly hair.

"Mom," I cried. Again I got choked up.

What was it with my emotions lately? I felt like a regular crying machine.

Mom picked up my tote bag and led me through the crowd. It was only then that I noticed the big white banner stretched across the room.

"Welcome home, Dawn!" it said.

Mary Anne was holding up one end of the banner, Claudia was holding up the other, and Kristy, Mallory, and Jessi were gathered underneath. It was the whole club!

"Surprise!" they cried.

In an instant, the banner was dropped and everyone was crowded around me, firing questions at me and hugging me hello.

"You're so *tan!*" Mary Anne cried.

She grabbed my arm and held it up for the others to see.

"Did you have a good time?" asked Claudia.

"Did you miss us?" asked Kristy.

"Tell us about We ♥ Kids," said Mallory.

"What was Disneyland like?" asked Jessi.

Phew! I couldn't answer everything at once, so I just stood there grinning. I dug into my tote bag and pulled out the five pairs of Mickey Mouse ears I had bought my friends as presents. Everyone grabbed for them and put them on right there in the airport.

We made our way to the baggage claim area, giggling and talking in a tight cluster. I guess we looked pretty funny. The people walking by smiled at us as they passed.

"We've got you signed up for some jobs," Mary Anne told me. Throughout the chaos, Mary Anne had stuck right by my side. "Hope you don't mind."

"Mind? That's great!" I said. Home just a few minutes and already I was booked. That was the Baby-sitters Club, all right. Bustling and busy.

When my suitcase came around on the carousel, Mom grabbed it up and the rest of us followed her out the automatic airport doors. She strode right to the parking lot, directly to the row where she had left the car.

"Here we are," she smiled, very pleased with herself. "Bet you thought your old mom would forget where she parked. My memory's getting better. Really. I'm making an effort."

We all piled in and I squeezed next to Mom. She steered the car to the ticket window and stopped to pay the charge.

The ticket. Mom fished into the pocket of her blouse. She grabbed her purse off the floor and rummaged through the various compartments. She looked through her wallet.

"Dawn," she said. "Will you check the glove compartment?"

No ticket.

"Maybe you stuck it behind the sun visor," I said.

She flipped the visor down. There was the ticket, tucked into the visor's pocket.

Mom handed the attendant his money and we drove out of the airport, onto the highway. As we sped home, I couldn't help smiling. My friends were chattering, my mom was Mom, and I was snug in the middle. I was home, all right. And it felt super.

About the Author

Ann M. Martin's The Baby-sitters Club has sold over 190 million copies and inspired a generation of young readers. Her novels include the Newbery Honor Book *A Corner of the Universe*, *A Dog's Life*, and the Main Street series. She lives in upstate New York.

Keep reading for a sneak peek at the next book
from The Baby-sitters Club!

Kristy and the Mother's Day Surprise

Dinner that night was noisy. It was one of the few times when everyone was home. Andrew and Karen usually aren't with us, and when they are, they're almost always here on a weekend — when Charlie's out on a date or Sam is at a game at school, or *something*. But that night was different. We ate in the dining room. Watson sat at one end of the table, Mom at the other. David Michael,

Karen, and I sat along one side of the table; Charlie, Sam, and Andrew sat across from us.

When everyone had been served, Mom said, "Isn't this nice?" She had been a little emotional lately.

"It's terrific," agreed Watson, who sounded *too* enthusiastic.

Mom and Watson get all worked up whenever we're together as a family, and I know why. I like my family and everything. I like us a lot. But sometimes I think we feel more like pieces of a family instead of a whole family. We're a shirt whose seams haven't all been stitched up. I mean, Mom and Watson got married, but I would only go to Mom if I needed to borrow money. And Andrew usually heads for Watson if he's hurt himself or doesn't feel well. *We're* Mom's kids and *they're* Watson's kids. Two teams on the same playing field.

Don't get me wrong. It isn't bad. Really. Our family just needs to grow together — so Mom and Watson make a huge deal out of things like all of us sitting down at the dinner table.

Our dinners are usually not very quiet. That night, David Michael started things off by singing softly, "*They built the ship* Titanic *to sail the ocean blue. A sadder ship the waters never knew. She was on her maiden trip when an iceboard hit the ship —*"

"Cut it *out!*" cried Karen suddenly. "I hate that song. All the people die. Besides, it's 'ice*berg,*' not 'ice*board.*'"

"I know that," said David Michael. But he didn't. He had said 'iceboard' every time he had sung that song.

He stopped singing. He made a rhythm band out of his plate, glass, fork, and spoon.

Andrew joined him.

Chink-a-chink. Chinkety-chink, chink.

Mom beamed. Why did she look so happy? Usually dinnertime rhythm bands gave her a headache.

"Hey, Karen. Your epidermis is showing," said Sam from across the table.

"What? What?" Karen, flustered, began checking her clothes. Finally, she said haughtily, "Sam. I am not wearing a dress. How can my epipotomus be showing?"

We couldn't help it. Watson, Mom, Charlie, Sam, David Michael, and I began to laugh. Not rudely, just gently. Well, all right. David Michael laughed rudely — loudly, anyway.

"What?" Karen demanded.

"It's 'epidermis,' not 'epipotomus,'" said David Michael, glad to be able to correct *her*, "and it means 'skin.'"

Karen looked questioningly at Sam.

"He's right," said Sam. "It does mean 'skin.' "

"My *skin* is showing?" said Karen. "Oh, my *skin* is showing! That's funny! I'm going to say that to everyone in my class tomorrow."

"Now let's have a little eating," said Watson.

For a few moments, we ate. I was working on a mouthful of lima beans when I heard David Michael murmur, *"Beans, beans, they're good for your heart. The more you eat, the more —"*

I kicked him under the table. Not hard. Just enough to make him stop. Mom and Watson *hate* that song.

But soon my brother was singing, *"Beans, beans, the magical fruit. The more you eat —"*

I kicked him again. "Cut it *out.*"

"It's a different song."

"Not different enough."

David Michael grew silent.

At her end of the table, Mom put down her fork and looked lovingly at Watson. "We're so lucky," she said.

Watson smiled.

I glanced at Sam and Charlie. Mom had been acting weird lately.

"We've got six beautiful children —"

"I am not beautiful," said David Michael. "I'm a boy."

"We live in a lovely town," continued Mom, "we like our jobs, we have a gorgeous house . . . with plenty of rooms. Do you realize that we have three spare bedrooms?"

My mother was looking at us kids.

I glanced at Sam and Charlie again. They shrugged.

"It *is* a nice house, Mom," I agreed.

Mom nodded. "Plenty of extra space."

Suddenly Sam said, "Hey, Mom, you're not pregnant, are you?"

(My mother *could* have been pregnant. She's only in her late thirties. She had Charlie right after she graduated from college.)

"No," Mom replied. "I'm not. . . . But how would you kids feel about another brother or sister?"

Oh. So she was trying to *become* pregnant.

"Another brother or sister?" David Michael repeated dubiously.

"A *baby*?" squeaked Andrew and Karen.

"Great!" said Sam and Charlie.

"Terrific!" I added honestly. I love babies. Imagine having one right in my house, twenty-four hours a day.

But the little kids just couldn't be enthusiastic.

"Why do you want a baby?" asked Karen bluntly.

"Oh, we didn't say we want a *baby* —" Watson began.

But before he could finish, Andrew spoke up. "A baby," he said, "would be the youngest person in the family. But that's *me*. *I'm* the youngest. I don't want a baby."

"Babies smell," added Karen.

"They cry," said David Michael. "And burp and spit up and get baby food in their hair. And you have to *change their diapers.*"

"Kids, kids," exclaimed Watson, holding his hands up. "Elizabeth just asked about another brother or sister, that's all."

Silence.

At last David Michael said, "Well, brothers and sisters start out as babies, don't they?"

And Andrew said, "I think we've got enough kids around here."

"Yeah," agreed Karen and David Michael.

But I couldn't help saying, "Another kid would be great. Really."

Sam and Charlie nodded.

No one seemed to know what to say then, but it didn't matter because Boo-Boo came into the dining room carrying a mole he'd caught, and we all jumped out of our chairs. The poor mole was still alive, so we had to get it away from Boo-Boo and then put it back outside where it belonged.

That was the end of dinner.

Want more baby-sitting?

ANN M. MARTIN #6

Boy-Crazy Stacey

ANN M. MARTIN #7

Claudia and Mean Janine

ANN M. MARTIN

The Ghost at Dawn's House

ANN M. MARTIN #10

Logan likes Mary Anne!

ANN M. MARTIN #11

Kristy and the Snobs

ANN M. MARTIN

Claudia and the New Girl

ANN M. MARTIN #13

Good-bye Stacey, Good-bye

ANN M. MARTIN

Hello, Mallory

ANN M. MARTIN

Little Miss Stoneybrook... and Dawn

ANN M. MARTIN #16

Jessi's Secret Language

And many more!

Don't miss any of the books in the Baby-sitters Club series by Ann M. Martin—available as ebooks

DON'T MISS
THE BABY-SITTERS CLUB
GRAPHIC NOVELS!

KRISTY'S GREAT IDEA

THE TRUTH ABOUT STACEY

MARY ANNE SAVES THE DAY

CLAUDIA AND MEAN JANINE

DAWN AND THE IMPOSSIBLE THREE

KRISTY'S BIG DAY

BOY-CRAZY STACEY

LOGAN LIKES MARY ANNE!

CLAUDIA AND THE NEW GIRL

AN IMPRINT OF

SCHOLASTIC

scholastic.com/graphix

BSC